JUST LIKE FATE

JUST LIKE FATE

Cat Patrick and Suzanne Young

Simon Pulse

New York London Toronto Sydney New Delhi

SIMON PULSE

An imprint of Simon & Schuster Children's Publishing Division
1230 Avenue of the Americas, New York, NY 10020
First Simon Pulse hardcover edition August 2013
Text copyright © 2013 by Cat Patrick and Suzanne Young
Jacket photographs copyright © 2013 by Getty Images
Jacket designed by Jessica Handelman
All rights reserved, including the right of reproduction in whole or in part in any form.
SIMON PULSE and colophon are registered trademarks of Simon & Schuster, Inc.
For information about special discounts for bulk purchases, please contact
Simon & Schuster Special Sales at 1-866-506-1949 or business@simonandschuster.com.
The Simon & Schuster Speakers Bureau can bring authors to your live event. For more
information or to book an event contact the Simon & Schuster Speakers Bureau
at 1-866-248-3049 or visit our website at www.simonspeakers.com.
Interior designed by Hilary Zarycky
The text of this book was set in Bulmer.
Manufactured in the United States of America
2 4 6 8 10 9 7 5 3 1
Library of Congress Cataloging-in-Publication Data
Patrick, Cat.
Just like fate / by Cat Patrick and Suzanne Young. — First Simon Pulse hardcover edition.
p. cm.
Summary: With her grandmother dying, Caroline is given a choice to either stay by her gram's side or go to the biggest party of the year. The story is told in alternating chapters, revealing what happens if Caroline stays or goes.
ISBN 978-1-4424-7271-6
[1. Fate and fatalism—Fiction. 2. Choice—Fiction. 3. Dating (Social customs)—Fiction.
4. Grandmothers—Fiction.] I. Young, Suzanne. II. Title.
PZ7.P2746Ju 2013
[Fic]—dc23
2012045071
ISBN 978-1-4424-7273-0 (eBook)

In loving memory of our grandmothers,
Josephine, Lora, and Mary,
who loved us no matter our choices

No trees in sight, just concrete
Still I see
Two roads twist and turn in front of me
No signs, but screams
Which way's reality?

So you choose; yeah, you choose
Maybe you lose
The sidewalk paved in hitches
Broken hearts not fixed by stitches
But morning's coming soon

No right in sight, just questions
And you find
There is no map to Mecca
It's just life
No right answer; perfect marks
It's no big deal; it's just your heart
Falling stars and lightning sparks
This will only sting a bit

We are all just
Magnets for fate
Stumbling, skipping, running at our pace
Making choices, losing voices
Making wishes for forgiveness
But morning's coming soon

And no matter where you sit, how fast you sip
The coffee tastes the same on magnet lips

"Magnets for Fate"
—Electric Freakshow

ONE

There are exactly sixteen minutes left in math class when there's a faint double knock on the classroom door, and we all perk up. Through the window I can see the office assistant with the frizzy hair standing timidly, like she's afraid of even herself.

We watch curiously as Mr. Pip lumbers over, wiping his perpetually sweaty forehead as he goes. He opens the door two feet at best, and I almost expect him to ask the woman in the hall for a secret password. She whispers something, then hands over a tiny piece of pink paper. I know that pink: It's a hall pass.

Someone's getting out of here early.

"Caroline Cabot, please report to the office," Mr. Pip says in his nasally voice. At the sound of my name, I drop the piece of strawberry-blond hair I'm twirling and, eyebrows furrowed, look across the aisle at Simone.

"What'd you do now, Linus?" she asks with a twinkle

in her dark eyes. The guy one row over wakes up when she speaks. Simone's like a half Asian Marilyn Monroe with Angelina Jolie lips—guys are constantly checking her out.

"You should talk," I say, reaching down to grab the backpack stuffed into the basket beneath my seat. "You're the one with the monogrammed chair in the principal's office." Simone's had detention three times this year already, but as far as the office is concerned, I'm a good girl.

On my way out, I look back at Simone and waggle my phone in her direction. She makes a face to acknowledge that texting me later is obvious just before I slip out of sight.

I think of detouring through the science wing for a glimpse of Joel, but the rule follower in me takes over and I head straight to see the principal. On my way there, I picture Joel and Lauren breaking up—maybe she has a fling with a guy her own age at the community college—and him falling madly in love with me. I laugh at myself as I push through the doors of the main office.

Then I see the look on Principal Jones's face.

Immediately I feel it: Something's wrong.

"Caroline," he says, his deep vibrato at odds with his soft expression. "Your mother called." He stops, motioning at the chair near the window. "Here, sit."

My stomach twists. Principal Jones is nothing short of intimidating, and this unprovoked kindness is like a flashing neon sign that reads BRACE YOURSELF. I slowly lower into the chair, even more alarmed when my principal turns to face me.

"Your grandmother's in the hospital," he says. "She had a stroke and your mother—"

I don't hear the rest because I lean forward, my head between my knees like there's an impending plane crash. My throat seizes, and I make a sound halfway between a moan and a whimper. I was just with my grandmother this morning, rolling my eyes when she told me to put my cereal bowl in the sink. *Why did I roll my eyes?*

"Is she okay?" I ask, tears coming faster than I can blink them away.

"I'm not clear on the details. But your mom said your brother would be here to pick you up and then—"

"I can't wait for him." I stand, pulling my backpack over my shoulders. "Which hospital?" Panic has my heart racing, my skin prickling. Principal Jones is stumbling over his words, but I don't have time for this. I have to see Gram. "St. Mark's?" I ask impatiently.

When he nods, I dash out of the office, not stopping even when the assistant calls after me from the front desk. I'm a bundle of fear loosely held together by purpose. As I jog through the empty halls, I take out my phone and text my brother.

DRIVING MYSELF. SEE YOU THERE.

. . .

The hospital is a massive maze, and at the very moment that I wonder how I'm ever going to find Gram, Natalie appears out of nowhere.

"Where's Teddy?" she says, grabbing my arm from behind like a mugger. My sister's wearing jeans, a black turtleneck sweater, and her dark-framed glasses. As usual, she looks more forty than almost twenty.

"I drove myself."

"You were supposed to wait for him," she snaps.

"Well, I didn't," I snap back. It'd be nice if our animosity were a result of the tension of the moment, but unfortunately this is our brand of sisterly love. Teddy is the older sibling who took me to R-rated movies before I turned seventeen; Natalie's the one who told on me for sneaking out. In a nutshell, she sucks.

"Where are we going?" I ask, looking around.

"Gram's on the third floor," Natalie says through permanently pursed lips. "Come on."

We ride the elevator in silence. When the doors open, my sister walks purposefully down one long corridor, around a corner, and down another. My stomach clenches tighter and tighter with each room we pass. I try not to look at the people inside—to wonder how many of them are dying.

I try not to wonder whether Gram's dying.

She was already weak from the chemo treatments she finished a few months ago. But she was better. The doctors assured all of us that she was better.

As warm tears run down my cheeks, I'm suddenly twelve years old again. I'm on my grandmother's front porch with a suitcase, asking if I can live with her. My parents' divorce is getting uglier by the day, and I don't want to be their pawn to hurt each other. I've opted out. And when Gram agrees, I am struck with relief and gratitude. She's always been my rock; I can't lose her.

"Here," Natalie says, gesturing toward a door open a crack. I nod and take a deep breath of antiseptic air, then follow her in. I can't help it: I gasp. Seeing Gram in a hospital bed is like a punch in the gut.

"Hi," I say, desperately trying to keep the despair out of my voice, the tears from my eyes. But when Gram raises a skinny, veiny arm and waves, I can't hold back. I rush to her bedside, crying the kind of tears that don't care if they make you look ugly.

"Stop that now, Caroline," Gram says, reaching out to hold my hand with the arm that's free from the IV. Her hand is the same one that makes me breakfast, but it feels alien. Cold. Frail. Even worse, her words are coming out funny—slurred somehow. She sounds like she's drunk. "I'm going to be fine," she says, but "fine" sounds like "fline."

"Yes," I say, knowing if I say more, I'll start blubbering again.

I'm still holding Gram's hand when Mom walks in with my little sister, Judith.

"Where's Teddy?" Mom asks when she sees me. Apparently, whether or not my brother is inconvenienced is what's really important here. The funny thing is that Teddy won't care—he's the most laid-back one of all of us.

"She didn't wait for him," Natalie mutters to Mom in that annoyingly soft voice she uses when she's only pretending to be discreet.

"Well, you're here now," Mom says, sighing at me.

"Coco!" Judith says, dropping Mom's hand and rushing toward me. She hugs my leg, and I squeeze her as best I can without letting go of Gram. I run my palm over her baby blond hair and smile.

"Hi, Juju," I say. "How are you?"

"Mama gave me juice," she says proudly. At two and a half, she's all belly and bum; she stands like an adorable troll doll, beaming at me. Then she looks at Gram. "We bringed you juice, too, Gamma!"

Judith runs over and grabs a juice box from Mom's gigantic purse, then returns to the bedside and tosses it up onto Gram's lap. Gram beams back at her. "How thoughtful of you," she says. "Thank you, Judith."

Julif.

I look away from Gram's face when I realize that one side is sagging lower than the other. Thankfully, a nurse comes in right then and says he needs to check her vitals.

"Let's all step out for a minute," Mom says, giving me a look that tells me I'm coming with her, whether I like it or not. "We'll go get a snack and be back in a few minutes, Mom."

"All right, then," Gram says, releasing my hand. It feels like I've just taken off my coat in a blizzard. I want to grab hold again, but the nurse has already moved in with his pushcart full of tools. "See you."

Sheeu.

I swallow down the lump in my throat and follow Mom, Judith, and Natalie out of the room. Teddy is walking toward us from the elevator, and when he joins our group, he's the only one on the face of the planet who manages not to give me crap about driving myself. Instead he nudges me with his elbow and whispers, "She'll be fine, Coco."

And that makes me cry all over again.

When Judith is preoccupied, hopping from tile to tile in the hallway, my mother talks in a detached voice. "I didn't want to say this in front of her, but they did a scan." Natalie's eyes are round as saucers and Teddy crosses his arms over his chest, listening intently. I feel light-headed.

Mom sighs heavily. "The cancer has spread. It's throughout her abdomen, her lungs. Her brain."

"Oh my God." It's all I can manage. Natalie reaches for my mother immediately. I look at Teddy as he shakes his head slowly.

"She's weak from the stroke, and the cancer is everywhere," Mom continues, letting go of Natalie. "The oncologist says she's too far gone—that there's nothing they can do but make her comfortable." My mother takes a deep breath and meets my eyes. "She doesn't have long."

I want to ask specifically how long that means. I want to ask why the chemo worked but then didn't. I want to ask a million things, but everything stills—even my vocal cords. In that quiet, my thoughts are noisy: I'm losing my confidant. I'm losing my best friend.

"Coco?" Teddy asks, like he said something before but I didn't hear him. It pulls me out. "Are you okay?"

"I don't know," I say. My ears are ringing.

"Do you want to sit down?" he asks, nodding to the chairs near the wall.

Natalie huffs, wiping the tears under her glasses. "It's always about you, isn't it," she murmurs.

The anger in my sister's voice lights a fire in me. I'm so sick of her telling me what to do, acting like I'm some inconvenience to the family. She's been like this ever since the divorce. I spin toward her, ready to strike back.

Teddy steps in before I tear into her. "Please," he says

to both of us. "I can't referee right now." His shoulders are hunched, and I realize that even my always-steady older brother is crumbling too. We fall silent and wait until the nurse leaves before crossing the hall. My mother pauses outside the doorway and turns to face us.

"Not a word about what I told you," she whispers. She grabs Judith's hand and walks back inside the room.

TWO

"Come out with me tonight," Simone says at the beginning of math. It's been three days since Gram was transferred from the hospital to the hospice facility—three excruciating days of me being forced to attend school when I should be there by Gram's side.

"You know I can't," I say seriously.

"You've gone every night this week," she protests. "You've become a slightly unwashed hermit."

"I still shower."

"Sure you do." She smiles, but when I don't laugh, she sighs. "Linus, I'm sure Gram will be feeling better soon."

I turn to her. "People don't get released from hospice," I say. "They're giving her drugs to make her comfortable. But she's still dying." *Too many drugs,* I think. *So many that half the time, she's out cold.*

"I'm sorry," she says softer, leaning in toward me because Mr. Pip looks like he's about to start class. "I'm not trying to sound insensitive. I just don't really know what to say anymore. No one close to me has ever been sick. You love your gram—hell, I love her too. But it's like you're fading away, Caroline. You're living at your mom's, sleeping in your weird old penguin bedroom—"

"Not by choice," I interrupt. "My mom won't let me stay at my *real* house. At Gram's."

"I know," Simone says, nodding. "And it sucks. Everything sucks for you right now. That's my point. Can't you take one night off? We'll do something fun. I hear there's a party at—"

"No," I say quickly, but without conviction. Then Mr. Pip gives us a look and we're forced to be quiet.

My eyes fall to my blank notebook. I feel heavy with guilt, like there's lead in my veins. Truth be told, I'd give anything to go to a party, no matter where it is. I'd give anything to get away from it all. I'm craving a break from my life. From my grief. From my family.

From Gram.

Because when it comes down to it, waiting for someone to die is like being told a tornado is coming. You press pause on your life and brace yourself—but you don't know when it will hit, how bad it'll be. You can prepare all you want, but in the end, you just don't know.

. . .

When I arrive at the hospice facility after school, Gram is asleep in the bed—but her face is slack, her chest rising and falling slowly. Natalie waits at her side, and she looks up with a weary expression, her hair in a messy knot.

"Where's Teddy?" I ask.

"He went to grab something to eat. It's exhausting being here all day." She says it like it's my choice to go to school, as if I wouldn't rather stay here with my grandmother, begging the universe to let me keep her. I pull up a chair on the other side of the bed and try to block out my sister's existence. It doesn't work.

"Her vitals were weak this morning," Natalie murmurs. "They've been adjusting her medication."

"Her vitals were weak two days ago, then they got better."

"Well, she's worse now," Natalie says. "She hasn't woken up all day, and they don't know when she will. Mom nearly collapsed and I had to call Albert to take her out for some air. She's going to need you after this, so don't pull one of your stunts."

I scoff. "Stunts? It was five years ago, Natalie. I had every right to move in with Gram." I lean toward my sister. "And I'm still glad I left. I don't regret a second of it." I sit back, feeling sick that Natalie brings out the venom in me.

"Where will you run away to this time?" she asks bitterly. "There's no one to pick up your pieces anymore."

I glance sideways at my grandmother's face, serene in sleep . . . or sedation. "She's not dead, you know," I whisper. "So stop acting like she is." I take Gram's hand, noting how cool her skin is. I stand and the chair scrapes loudly on the floor. "I'm not going to sit here listening to this," I tell Natalie. "Have Teddy call me when he gets back."

I walk away, feeling my sister's glare on my back. "That's right, Caroline," she calls out dramatically. "Run away. Take all the attention for yourself. You're worse than the two-year-old because you should know better."

"Drop dead," I say, and then suddenly wish I could take it back. I turn to my sister, her expression stunned and hurt, but it's too late to apologize. Instead I can only lower my eyes.

"Love you, Gram," I tell my grandmother, hoping she can hear me. And then I leave, planning to come back when Teddy does. Just as I get into the hallway, the sunlight outside the window fades behind a cloud, making it seem suddenly dark. It's eerie even though I'm safe. My phone rings, startling me. I glance at the caller ID and take a deep breath.

"Hey," I say into the line.

"Well?" Simone asks. "Are you coming with me or do I have to kidnap you? Please tell me it's the first option, because I'm running low on chloroform." She launches into a description of the party, who will be there, and what her outfit options are.

"It's not a good time, Mony," I say, interrupting her. "My sister is a rag and my mother is having a breakdown. I swear to God if Teddy falls apart, I might just lose it completely."

"Maybe you need some space from your family." She says it as if she actually believes the words and isn't just trying to bend me to her will. "One night off. Come on, Linus. Don't make me forge important high school memories alone."

I smile, thinking it over. A party—a college party—sounds like a truly good time, the sort of good time we'll talk about for the rest of the year. Then again, these moments with my grandmother could be the last I have.

"So . . . ," Simone says, waiting for my decision. "Are you going to spend the evening with me and distinguished alumni, or are you going to argue with your sister all night?"

It might be my imagination, but the hallway seems to darken even more. No one is around, and for one moment everything is quiet. And then I sigh.

"Simone," I start, my decision made. "I'm going to—"

THREE

STAY

"—stay."

Simone's quiet; I know she doesn't understand. She's never experienced anything like what I'm going through. I think of reconsidering—it's just one night—but once the decision's made, my shoulders loosen. Even though Gram seems the same, and as much as I don't want to be anywhere near Natalie, there's no way I'm leaving tonight.

"Fine," Simone says. "But don't come crying to me, Argentina, when you're the only one without a superhot college boyfriend tomorrow."

"Promise," I say with a forced laugh. *The guy I like is our age anyway.* "Call you later?"

"You'd better," Simone says. "I'm sure I'll have all sorts of scandalous gossip. You know how Gwen and Felicity are when they're around older guys."

"Total Lolita-land," I say, laughing for real. "Remember the time with the water bra?" Simone snorts, which makes me laugh harder. When we stop, she surprises me with sincerity.

"Take care of yourself, Linus," she says quietly. "We all know how much you love Gram—just remember to love *you*, too."

"I will," I say, forcing the words past the lump in my throat. "I'll try."

As I hang up the phone, the light in the hall returns—the fluorescent bulbs and white walls are all their normal boring colors again.

I walk back to Gram's room. A nurse is checking her vitals while Natalie's sitting awkwardly on the very front of the recliner near the window, like she doesn't want to risk getting too comfortable. It occurs to me that it's like a metaphor for her entire life.

"Is your mother coming back soon?" the nurse asks in a clipped tone that makes me nervous.

"Yes," Natalie answers. "She just went out for some air. I can call her?" Nat looks at me, and I see the anxiousness in her eyes too.

"I think that'd be a good idea," the nurse says. "Just in case your grandmother wakes up."

In case she wakes up?

Before I have time to ask about the alternative—Gram *not* waking up—the nurse briskly leaves the room.

Panicked, I turn to Natalie. I don't know how or why, but I see my sister in that moment—really *see* her. She's got a tough outer shell, but she's loyal to those she loves. And one of the people she loves the most is dying. We are the same, she and I. For the first time in a long while, I go and sit next to her.

"I don't want to fight," I say quietly. My mouth is dry, and I'm actually nervous to be having this conversation. It strikes me as strange—after all, she's my *sister*. "I don't think I can fight anymore."

Natalie's surprised eyes find mine, but she doesn't say anything. I continue. "Gram's been there for me, but I'm starting to realize that she won't always be. And I'm scared." My face stings with the start of a cry, and I turn to find Natalie watching me with a softened expression.

"I don't want to fight either," she says. "I'm sorry, Caroline. I really am." She's never told me she was sorry. Never. I let the words linger in the air to unravel the hurt they've caused all this time. I didn't know how badly I needed to hear them.

"I don't know how we got so . . . ," I begin, not sure what word to use.

"It was my fault," Nat says.

"But I made it worse," I say, shaking my head. "I'm sorry."

Natalie shifts uncomfortably. She's never been good at letting people in. For a while, I thought that if only Nat had my back a bit more, I might've stayed at home after the divorce.

But that's just not her . . . not since we were little anyway.

Under normal circumstances—like if this were Teddy or Simone or even Mom—I'd reach out for a hug. Instead I keep my hands folded in my lap.

Gram is dying. I close my eyes for a moment, wishing it weren't true, but when I open them again, there she is— motionless on the bed.

Slipping away.

THREE

GO

"Simone," I start, my decision made. "I'm going to . . . go. I'll go with you to the party, but only because I can't stand another minute with my sister. I swear she waits for me to screw up just so she can throw it back in my face."

"If Natalie's going to be a jerk all night," Simone says, "you shouldn't have to deal with it."

I nod, thinking about how many times my sister has belittled me, made me feel like I'm not a part of my own family.

"And really," Simone adds, "if she's going to complain anyway, why not give her something good to work with?" I can hear the smile in her voice, challenging and protective as a best friend should be. As a sister should be.

"Yeah," I say, looking back toward the room. "Why not." I lean against the wall and exhale. "Hey, would you mind picking me up?" I ask. "That way when you drop me off tonight,

I can stop in and say good-bye—*good night* to Gram." I pause, thinking how different the word "good-bye" is now. How much heavier it is in my mouth.

"Simone?" I ask hesitantly. "Gram will be okay if I leave, right?"

"Of course she will be. It's just a few hours."

A feeling of dread comes over me, but the light in the hall returns—the fluorescent bulbs and white walls are all their normal boring colors again. In a way, it allows me to push away my concern and realize that Simone's right—it's just one night out of all the nights I've been by my grandmother's side. If she were awake, she would probably tell me to go to the party. She'd tell me to wear lipstick, too. And a night away from Natalie can never be a bad thing.

"I'm on my way," Simone says. "We'll grab burgers or something first."

I agree, but when we hang up, nervousness creeps up my arms. I'm not a fan of confrontation, and this looming one with my sister is going to be a blowout.

The nurse is just leaving Gram's room when I get back. I see Natalie hovering near the window, back straight, mouth downturned. I cross my arms over my chest, feeling the rift between my sister and me growing. I wonder if eventually it'll get big enough to end our relationship altogether.

The minute I step into the room, her judging eyes find

me. "Where'd you go?" she asks. "I just got done talking to Mom."

"I was busy," I say, reaching for Gram's hand. Her skin is thin and pale, her lips slightly parted in unconsciousness. As I hold her, I have the fleeting thought that this is it. I want to tell my grandmother everything I'm thinking and feeling. I want to tell her that I love her. Absently I bring her palm to my cheek, imagining that she's awake, saying how much she loves me, too. When tears flood my eyes, I sniffle and set Gram's hand back down. *It's only a few hours,* I tell myself. *And maybe then Natalie will be gone and I can hang with Gram—just the two of us, like it's supposed to be.*

"I'm going out," I say to my sister, not looking in her direction. "Tell Mom I'll be home after eleven."

"What? You can't just . . ." She jumps up from the chair. "You're so goddamn selfish, Caroline," she says. "Do you think you can just do whatever you want? You have an obligation to this family. You—"

"Oh, shut up!" I call out, my voice carrying through the sparse room. "You're not my mother—you're certainly not Gram. Maybe if you had your own life, you wouldn't—"

"Don't you dare!" she shouts. "I've been the one to hold this family together. I'm the one who makes sure Mom eats her dinner when she can't stop crying." My sister puts her hand over her mouth as if she's afraid she might betray an actual emotion other than bitch. After a second, she shakes her head. "You know what, go. Go, you coward."

I'm shaking I'm so angry, so hurt. I can't even think of something to say, can only grab my backpack and race out of there. I'm halfway down the hall when I realize I didn't tell Gram that I love her, didn't kiss her cheek good night. But I can't face my sister, so I vow to tell Gram twice later.

FOUR

STAY

I'm still with my sister, staring at the muted news on TV as an awkward, post-apology silence fills the space between us. My mother and my stepdad, Albert, return to the room, but my mother looks like a piece of ripped paper that someone hastily taped back together. She's got that shiny redness to her face that happens when you cry off your makeup, and her hair's fluffy-weird like she combed out what had been hair sprayed before. Seconds later, as if it were choreographed, Teddy walks in with two greasy bags from Burger Barn.

We dive on him like a pack of wild dogs, and just as Nat takes the biggest bite in history, Aunt Claudia breezes in wearing all black with a hot pink pashmina on top. Her bracelets and necklaces clink and clank, even at her slightest movements.

My mother immediately tenses. Aunt Claudia is her older

sister. She's a manless, kidless career woman who lives by business books. She frowns whenever she looks at me like I'm the visual representation of my mother's bad choices in life.

Natalie idolizes her.

"Hi, Aunt Claudia!" Nat says, mouth full.

"Hello, darling," Claudia says, managing to side hug Natalie while still staying far enough away not to get smeared with mustard or calories. She turns to my mother. "Diane," she says. "You're looking . . ." Her voice trails off; she doesn't bother to lie.

"Nice of you to join us," Mom says, her words dripping with accusation. I watch them, and like earlier with Natalie, I can *see* them. How my aunt Claudia talks down to my mother. How my mother lets her.

Aunt Claudia startles me from my thoughts as she appears in front of me. "You can't say hello?" she asks with a chilly smile. Teddy speaks for both of us when he asks how she is.

My aunt doesn't answer. Instead she turns, like she's been waiting to look the entire time, and stares at my grandmother lying in the bed. My aunt's proud shoulders sag slightly, her body seeming to wilt at the sight of her mother dying. But then she straightens and glides across the room to sit next to her.

"Hi, Ma," she says softly, touching her arm. We're all quiet until I hear my mother sniffle, and then Aunt Claudia looks over, stoic as usual.

"How long does she have?" she asks. "I'll need to know whether to reschedule my flight to Cleveland."

Mom, who's never been about anyone but family her entire life—maybe to a fault—stares at her sister with her mouth open. Then she shakes her head slowly from side to side, like she's about to lose it. I freeze with a half-mushed french fry between my teeth, wondering what'll happen next.

"You callous—" my mother starts.

And that's when Gram speaks.

"Stop fighting," she says, blinking her eyes open. "I don't want those to be the last words I hear." Her speech reminds me of Judith's—babylike.

Gram's eyelids droop as if it's a struggle to keep them open at all. We all jump up as my mother and Aunt Claudia crowd around her.

I grab Teddy's arm—relief washes over me. *She woke up.* I nearly start crying when Gram coughs, gritty and thick. My mother tries to help her sit up, but my grandmother waves her away.

"It's my time, Diane," Gram says. "It's just my time."

My brother darts a look at me, his face ghost pale. He touches my hand where I'm gripping his arm. "It's the medication," he reassures me. "She's out of it."

"No, I am not, Theodore," my grandmother says, matter-of-fact. Natalie actually takes a step back; she looks like she might hurl right on the white-tiled floor. "But I'm not going to sit and waste my last breath when you can't even get along at my deathbed."

"Ma," Aunt Claudia starts to say, when my grandmother turns to her. They both pause, an unspoken mother-daughter look passing between them. The tears in Aunt Claudia's eyes brim over, and my grandmother reaches to brush her hair back, the same way she's done for me a million times.

"Let me talk to the kids," Gram says quietly, gentle words that make my aunt look down. She waits for a minute, then leans to kiss Gram's cheek before walking out. My mom, stunned and devastated that she has to leave, can't seem to move until Albert comes over to take her elbow. He guides her from the room, and when she looks back, my gram winks at her.

I can't help it—I start to sob.

"Take her outside, Teddy," Gram says. "I want to talk to Natalie for a minute."

My brother puts his arm around me and forces me to the door; I turn and watch Natalie as she goes to lay her head on Gram's shoulder.

"Now, hush," Gram says, brushing her hair.

Their moment is private, intimate. I feel like I'm peeking

into a relationship I didn't know they had, and I'm jealous. I'm jealous that Gram didn't ask for me first.

"Come on, Coco," Teddy says, pulling me out. And when the door shuts behind us, I'm suddenly adrift in my loneliness as I wait for my grandmother's last words, hoping that she lasts long enough to give them to me.

FOUR

GO

I'm staring listlessly out the passenger window as Simone pulls onto Dover Street. The radio is blaring Electric Freakshow; Felicity and Gwen sing along—purposely off-key—in the back. I check my phone to see if anyone has texted from the hospital, but no one has. I'm suddenly so alone—even in a car filled with my friends.

"Check it out, Linus." Simone has to shout over the music. I turn to look out the windshield and immediately groan. Cars line both sides of the street, all leading up to a house that might as well have a banner that reads PLEASE CALL THE COPS. We drive by once looking for parking, earning a few catcalls from the lawn dwellers, then turn around and try again.

"I'm pretty sure you said *low-key* college party when you picked me up," I say, looking pointedly at Simone.

"Did I?" she asks innocently, avoiding my glare. The day

has gone dark, but there are only a few stars out. The sky is strange tonight, and I can't help but feel strange too.

I'm suddenly nervous, even though the party doesn't look exactly *wild*. There's a dude wearing a plaid sweater-vest, kicking a hacky sack in the driveway. And yet the hairs on the back of my neck stand up. I check my phone again. Nothing.

We end up parking three blocks away, a fact that Felicity complains about the whole time we walk through the crisp October air. Gwen nearly kills herself in the spike-heeled boots she's wearing, and when she's not groaning about the "hike," Felicity chatters on about looking for a quality guy. She calls dibs on the sweater-vest.

Although Simone and I have been hanging out with them since last year, it's pretty clear this is more of a convenience friendship than anything. Lunches and parties—that's about the extent of our interactions. I'm not close to them like I am with Simone. She and I are forever.

Just then Simone loops her arm through mine. "Guess who I heard will be here tonight?" She doesn't wait for me to answer. "Joel."

My stomach flips. "That's nice," I say, trying not to give anything away. But her laugh echoes down the street.

"Oh, yes. It is *very* nice. And from what I hear, Lauren is currently out of town visiting family." I abruptly stop walking, nearly pulling Simone's arm from its socket. Felicity and

Gwen keep going, calling back that they'll meet us inside. When Simone turns to me, I stare her down.

"You knew this all along, didn't you?" I ask, narrowing my eyes. "Is that why we're really here?"

Simone's red-stained lips pull into a broad smile. "It's not like your longing looks in Joel Ryder's direction have gone unnoticed. Don't ever say I never did anything for you, Linus." She smacks a kiss on my cheek and walks up the driveway to the house, giving the sweater-vest a teasing whistle as she passes. He salutes in response.

As I stand watching after her, listening to the sounds of muffled music leaking from the front door, my thoughts turn back to Gram.

I would do anything for her. Anything in the world. But instead of sitting at her side, I'm here at a party. I can't help but think that maybe my sister is right—I am selfish. I sigh heavily.

You're here; make the most of it, I think, rationalizing that I'll be back with Gram in a few hours. I lift my chin and walk inside.

There's a couple standing inside the entry, blocking my way as they argue over whether or not he was checking out his ex. I clear my throat and quietly say "excuse me," but neither budges. Simone gets farther down the hall and I try to interrupt again, this time earning a glare from the girlfriend. I've started to wonder if I'll be stuck in the breezy entryway for the rest of my life when I feel someone push in behind me.

"Excuse you," I say, holding up a palm to stop from being flattened between the door and the wall. The pusher—a blond, blue-eyed typical college random—looks at me in surprised amusement.

"I'm sorry. I didn't see you there," he says, too earnest to be serious. "It's just that sometimes I don't know my own superhuman strength." Just to prove it, he pretends to crash through the door—mouthing explosions and slow-motion roars—before shutting it gently behind him.

I can't help it; I laugh. "Forgiven," I say. "But they might be your kryptonite." I motion to the couple, who have now reached complete breakdown status. "Good luck getting past them. They're like the bouncers from hell." The guy glances at them, sizing up the situation before taking a spot against the closed door next to me.

"This might take a while," he says. "From what I hear, Jared there is still into his ex. Gertrude isn't pleased."

"You know them?" I ask.

He meets my eyes. "Uh, no. Do *you* know any Gertrudes? It's a fairly uncommon name. Wait, that's not your name, is it?"

I move closer to the wall, putting a little more space between me and Mr. Hilarious. "I think you're just trying to find out my name," I say.

"Busted. Well?"

The couple in front of us finally stops talking and instead embraces in what can only be described as a make-up hug, one with roaming hands and whispers. I start to worry that I'll somehow get sucked into their vortex of drama when my new friend murmurs next to me.

"Looks like Gerdy forgives him. It's sweet really. Such a bright future, those two."

"Yeah, well. I don't think she'll be as sweet to his ex, Belinda. After all, they used to be best friends."

The guy beams. "Belinda was a really good choice."

I laugh and then move ahead, finally getting past the couple as their make up turns make out. I'm scanning the room for Simone when the guy touches my shoulder.

"Do you need help finding someone?" he asks. "I know most of the girls here."

"Is that so?" I smile, lifting my eyebrow.

"Oh . . . no," he says quickly. "I don't mean I *know them* know them. . . . Well, maybe some of them . . ." When I playfully cross my arms over my chest as if waiting for him to go on, he tosses back his head and laughs. "Wow, my attempts at flirtation are going really well, don't you think? Wonder if I can make it any worse."

"I have faith in you."

He bites his lip, looking both embarrassed and exhilarated by our little exchange. I take the moment to check him out, noting that with his stupidly adorable smile, he probably has no problem meeting girls at parties.

"Chris!" someone yells to him from across the room. The guy lifts his chin in acknowledgment, but then turns like he's about to ask me something. Before he can, Simone appears out of nowhere and pulls me away.

"He's in the backyard," she says impatiently, not noticing the handsome blond who was about to . . . well, I don't know what he was about to do. But it must not have been that important because when I turn back to look, he's gone.

"Who's in the yard?" I ask, following behind Simone like a puppy dog. She turns abruptly.

"Joel," she says. "He's in the backyard—without Lauren. Are you going to talk to him or secretly pine away for the rest of your life? This isn't *Pride and Prejudice*, Keira Knightley."

"You know that was a book before it was a movie, right?"

Simone rolls her eyes. "Of course I know that. But it doesn't change the fact that the movie was ten times better. Now let's not leave poor Joel defenseless in a party full of Felicitys."

The full impact of her words hits, and a shock of nervous electricity races through me. Even though Simone let me borrow a cute, party-friendly outfit, I'm still in no condition to approach Joel. I might need to have a "Don't chicken out!" pep talk with my reflection. "I'll be right back," I tell Simone.

She sags dramatically against the hallway wall like she's completely inconvenienced. "Hurry," she sings.

My heart is thumping: The possibility of talking—actually talking—to Joel is a bit intimidating. It's not like I've never spoken to him before, but it's never been with the sole intent of ripping him from his girlfriend's clutches. God, I'm so embarrassed for myself. And even so, I take my place in the back of the bathroom line at the top of the stairs.

"We meet again," the guy from earlier says as he looks back from two people ahead of me. "We're on the same orbit tonight. And sorry about—"

My phone vibrates in my pocket, and the party fades into the background. The people. The music. Gone. Somehow I just know. I know even before I see that it's Teddy calling.

"Hello?" I answer, gripping the phone tightly.

"Hurry."

It's all my brother has to say before I'm trampling down the stairs, grabbing Simone by the shirtsleeve, and pulling her out the door.

FIVE

STAY

I sit next to Teddy, my head on his shoulder, in the hospice waiting room. My mother cries softly into my stepdad's button-down dress shirt. I stare at them, wondering if the last of Mom's makeup will be smeared on the white fabric, the little bits of normalcy of her appearance washed away with tears.

My aunt faces the window, across the room from any of us—on her own island. Just then, I hear the scraping of shoes and look up to see Natalie walk in.

Her face is red and blotchy, but her back is straight, her eyes determined. I'm alarmed at how . . . *right* she looks. I have this irrational hope that my grandmother is somehow fine. That she's cured and waiting to go home. But then my sister turns to my brother and says it's his turn.

"I'll be right back, okay?" Teddy says, untangling himself from me. "Keep it together, Caroline." His voice is serious, but in his expression I see impatience. He wants his time with Gram too. So I just nod and let him walk away.

Natalie doesn't take his place. Instead she walks over to kneel in front of my mother, whispering to her. My mom then turns to cry on her, reminding me that they have a bond I don't. Or at least one that I won't have once Gram is gone. I wait, and it's just a few minutes later when my brother comes out. His voice is broken from crying, and—unable to bear seeing his face—I don't look up at him.

"Hurry," he says. I stand and start toward Gram's room, hands shaking, heart about to burst.

I shut the door and walk to the chair next to Gram's bedside. She's lying there, her eyes closed, and all at once I think that maybe it's too late. I've already lost her. I stare down, relieved when I see her chest rising and falling.

I drop back into the chair next to her, banging my knees on the metal workings of the bed. I don't even wince, only lean closer to Gram. Her head rolls to the side, and she opens her eyes to look at me. She's suddenly so old—lost in her own skin.

"Caroline, at last," she says weakly. "My favorite."

I cover my mouth as hot tears spill over my cheeks—sobs shake my body. She watches me with weary eyes, eyes just like my mother's.

"We've always taken care of each other, you and I," she says. "But now you'll have to take care of yourself."

"But I want you," I say like I'm a child. "I can't do it without you."

She smiles gently. "You tend to the things at home for me," she says. "Walk the cat, water the flowers."

"I will." My grandmother's cat, Junior, walks on a leash and hates everyone but her. He's a menace, but when I asked her last year to get rid of him, she said he'd only leave when she did. Back then I never even thought it was a possibility.

Gram reaches to run the backs of her cool fingers over my cheek, and I clutch her shoulder like I can hold her to this earth. "Don't ever give up on yourself," she says. "Life is hard sometimes, and I'm sorry I won't be here for you." A tear slides over her temple.

"I'm scared," I say.

"Shh," she says. "Don't be afraid. I'm not. We all die." Her words give me chills. I swallow hard as her breaths become uneven. "Try to make good choices, but when you make a bad one, learn from it and move on."

"Gram—"

"And be careful who you love, Caroline," she whispers. "Never let them take too much. Never let them take what's *you*."

I nod, not fully getting her meaning but wanting to encourage her to go on. To keep talking. But Gram just stares at me for a second, smiling softly until her mouth goes slack.

"I love you," she says finally. It's so quiet, it's barely there at all.

"I love you more," I return, a stillness coming over me—a thick crushing pressure that's about to destroy me. Because as we stare at each other, I watch the life fade from my grandmother's eyes. And then she exhales one more time, long and deep . . . letting go.

FIVE

GO

My grandmother is dead.

I stumble from the hospice, my body on autopilot—empty and numb at the same time. The conversation I just had with Teddy is on repeat, cruelly infecting me with regret and shame. I get in my car and start driving, words in my head swirling in dark, black spirals.

The room is bare—Gram is gone, a single rose on her pillow instead. My brother's bloodshot eyes find me. He's destroyed.

"Did she wake up?" I ask him, scared of the answer. If she didn't wake, it means that she never got the chance to say good-bye. And if she did, I wasn't there. What did she think?

"Caroline," my brother says, looking away. Caroline. *The use of my full name breaks me.*

"Did she ask for me, Teddy?" My voice is high and frantic. My brother's eyes glass over and he nods before wiping hard at his face.

"It's not your fault," he says quietly.

It's not your fault.

It's not your fault.

It's like an echo in my brain as I push harder on the accelerator, fleeing the family I can't face. I've just lost the most important person in the world, and I wasn't there. I stare at the road ahead, thinking that my sister was right: There's no one left to pick up my pieces.

I drive aimlessly, looking for a distraction. The radio blasts music, but the words are only screeches of noise. I don't realize where I am until I see the rows of cars outside the party house. I try Simone's phone, but it goes to voice mail. Then I try again. Voice mail again. I can't help it, but I resent her for it. I slam my phone down on the seat and search for her car among the others.

I didn't get to say good-bye.

I want to replay the entire night, make a different choice. But I know there aren't any second chances. I screwed up. I ruined everything.

Simone's car is nowhere to be found and I feel the panic start to seep in, threatening me as it waits to take me over completely. I drive by the party once again, debating going inside—even though the thought of it turns my stomach. I see an open space right in front and go to swing in, but I have to brake fast before I nearly crush a guy sitting on the curb, hidden from view. He looks up, shielding his eyes from my headlights. It's the blond guy from earlier, and he stands so I can pull into the space.

Once parked, I click off my lights and roll down the passenger window. "What are you doing?" I call to him. "I could have run over your foot or something." He ducks down, looking in before smiling.

"You came back for me." He grins, but when I don't smile, his expression falters. "I got ditched," he says. "My friend was parked here, but he left with some girl. I thought maybe he'd remember he brought me and swing back through. Guess not."

I don't care, I think. *I don't care about anything.* I glance past the guy to the party house, people still on the lawn holding hands or holding cups as I sit in my car, wishing I never came here tonight.

"So . . . ," the guy says. "Are you getting out?" He's standing there in his white thermal shirt, his pulled-from-the-floor jeans. Everything about him looks easy and carefree. I can't even imagine what that's like anymore.

"I don't think so," I say quietly. He takes a step closer, resting his elbow on the top of the car as he stares in, getting a closer look at me. Then his mouth falls open.

"Oh my God," he says. "Are you okay?"

I catch my reflection in the rearview mirror and see that my mascara has run. I swipe under my eyes and then wipe the inky black on Simone's skirt. When I'm done I turn to the guy, thinking he's the only person who even cares how I am right now. "What's your name?" I ask.

He seems caught off guard. "It's Christopher . . . uh, Chris."

"The answer is no, Christopher," I tell him with a pathetic shrug. "I'm not okay. Not at all."

He looks me over, confused, concerned. Rather than press me further about my disheveled state, he nods toward the house. "We should skip the party, then," he says. "It's lame anyway. Maybe we can go grab a coffee? I know a place still open."

I lean my head back against the seat, utterly lost. I can't go sit in a well-lit café talking to a stranger when I'm not even sure where I'll sleep tonight. "I can't," I tell him. "I have to go."

"Again?" he asks quickly. "Is it me? I can certainly tone it down."

"It's not you." I debate telling him the rest and then opt not to. "And I'm sorry that . . ." I'm sorry for so many things that I can't even finish the sentence. I switch the car into gear, but I haven't even eased off the brake before Christopher is talking fast.

"Listen," he says. "Is there any chance you could give me a ride to my friend's house? He's not coming back, and to be honest, the only reason I didn't call a cab in the first place was because I was hoping I'd bump into you again." He smiles sheepishly, maybe embarrassed for having admitted it. "And look," he says softer. "We did. It's kind of like fate, right?

I look doubtfully at Christopher, not sure if I should give him a lift. I'm eventually going to have to answer to my family; I'm just not brave enough yet. But I'm not brave enough to be alone either. So after a quick nod, I unlock the car door for him to get in.

The starless sky is unsettling as I drive through the darkened neighborhood toward the freeway. The houses pass in blurs of porch lights, and I've nearly forgotten where we're headed when Christopher starts playing with the air vents.

"Christopher . . . ," I start.

"It's just Chris," he interrupts. "Only my nana and my family physician call me Christopher anymore. Maybe a professor or two. I'm a freshman at Clinton State, in case you're curious."

I glance sideways. That's the same college Teddy goes to in the next town over, a college I've visited at least a dozen times. "Do you know Teddy Cabot?" I ask, wondering if he'll tell my brother he saw me at a party right after my grandmother died. And wondering if my brother would be sickened by the thought.

"Doesn't ring a bell," Chris says. "Sounds handsome, though. Should I be jealous?"

"No," I say, relieved and a little grossed out by the joke. "He's my brother."

"Interesting. Is he the overprotective type?"

"I don't know," I tell him. "He's never needed to be." Teddy has always stuck up for me. He's never judged me—at least not yet. But what does he think now? How can he defend me after what I've done?

Chris grows restless and begins to tap his thumb on his thigh like a fidgety child. "Did you think the weather was weird today?" he asks. "I totally dorked out with a few friends and we"—finger quotes—"*borrowed* a telescope from the science building to watch the cloud patterns. It was pretty cool."

When I don't respond, Chris adjusts the passenger seat, sliding and reclining it until he's almost in the backseat. He looks like he's settling in for the night. "You're not laughing at any of my jokes," he says. "I'm debating whether or not you want me to shut up, but I feel wholly compelled to impress you."

When I look over, he smiles broadly, and I think that he's the exact kind of cute that I could fall for—if my heart wasn't already broken. I turn away. We reach the stoplight of an intersection, and Chris reaches to turn down the music.

"I know it's none of my business," he says in a quiet voice, "but why were you crying earlier?"

The light turns green, but I don't move. I'm frozen by the

emotions flooding me, threatening to rip me to shreds in front of him. I can't say it out loud. Finally I compose myself and drive a few blocks.

"You'll need to make a right here," he says, sounding defeated. I ease my foot on the gas, making the turn.

"My grandmother died," I whisper. It feels like saying it can make it happen all over again.

"I'm so sorry," Chris says. "When?"

"Tonight."

"Oh." It's a stunned word, a sad one. Chris looks out the window. And now I'm the one who can't handle the silence.

"We're not leaving the state, are we?" I ask him, filling the void. "Because I'm pretty sure I've crossed four county lines already."

"Why? You want to make a run for it, Thelma."

Despite all that's weighing me down, I choke out a small laugh.

"That was a laugh," he says, pointing at me. "Sure, it was a pathetic one, but it means all is not lost. I'm still impressive."

I fight back my smile. "Which way, Christopher?" He starts giving directions, and I turn left down a residential street.

"It's around here somewhere," he says under his breath.

I look over at him. "Are you telling me that you *don't know* where your friend lives?"

"Of course I know," he says. "It's just that at night, all the streets look the same. But it's definitely in this neighborhood. I remember that old church on the corner."

I groan and slow down to ten miles per hour as he studies the houses on one side, then the other. He snaps his fingers, startling me.

"I just realized that you never told me your name," he says. "What is it?"

"Caroline."

"That's pretty."

"Thanks."

"And sweet." He's quiet, but the minute he opens his mouth, I interrupt.

"You're not going to break into 'Sweet Caroline,' are you?"

He abruptly closes his mouth and shakes his head no. When I see that it's nearly eleven and Simone still hasn't returned my calls, I feel abandoned. And then I wonder if this is how Gram felt in her last moments.

"Wait, there it is," Chris says, motioning to the left side. "The one with the truck in the driveway." He scoffs. "See. I knew exactly where it was."

I pull to the curb, letting the engine idle as Chris checks for his wallet and keys. When he's done—taking way longer than necessary—he clears his throat. "Do you think I can call you sometime?" he asks.

There's a weird twist of excitement and sadness mixed together as I look at him. "Are you hitting on me five minutes after I told you that my grandmother died?" I ask.

He winces. "Wow, I'm a douche, huh?" He says it so innocently that I have to smile, even though I feel like a traitor for the gesture. Chris runs his hand through his hair, embarrassment painting his cheeks pink in the light of the streetlights.

"You're fine," I say. "It's me. I'm running a little high on the bitch-o-meter tonight. I'm not myself." I look down. "I don't know if I ever will be again."

"I really am sorry about your grandmother, Caroline," Chris says in his most serious tone of the night. I mean to look at him, to thank him, but I'm afraid if I do, I'll give him the wrong idea. And I can't be that selfish—not this time.

"You seem really great," I tell him. "I'm just not in a good place. My life's a mess, and you deserve better than that."

"That's possibly the nicest rejection I've ever gotten," Chris says, soft but playful. "So thank you for that." He opens the door and climbs out. Under different circumstances, I would have given him my number. Just not tonight.

"Well, Caroline," he says as he holds up his hand in a wave. "Sweet Caroline. It was a pleasure meeting you—officially. Maybe next time I'll get that number."

There's a small panic that I may never see him again, and so despite my vow to not lead him on, I smile. "Tell you what, if I ever happen to randomly run into you when I'm not crying and miserable, the digits are all yours."

Chris grins. "I'll hold you to that." And then he closes the door and jogs up the driveway.

SIX

STAY

I wake up on Saturday, the morning after the worst day of my life so far, and my sister's asleep next to me. I don't know when she came in, but I'm surprised to find that I don't mind that she's here. Whatever changed between us at the hospital seems to be still in effect, and having her here is like a silent peace treaty after years at war. Except that her presence reminds me of the reality that Gram's dead.

I don't move; I don't even feel like I'm breathing. I listen to the erratic drum of rain hitting the gutter outside, trying to force my thoughts away from Gram. They land on wondering whether the back window of my car is still cracked open from when Felicity thought she was going to puke after lunch yesterday. I wonder if it was cracked when I went to see—

Gram's dead.

It hits me again: the helplessness and the heartache. I

actually put my hand to my chest; I feel like I'll never take a deep breath again. But still, I don't cry. *Why don't I cry?*

I think of the way she looked just before she died. I think of standing by her bedside, listening to her talk. Those will be the last things she ever says. The thought makes my stomach tighten like a fist.

To calm myself, I think of all the mundane things I still have to do. Like walking a cat. "Freaking Junior," I mutter.

"What?" Natalie says, her voice groggy.

"Sorry," I say quietly. I slip out of the bed. "Go back to sleep." I gather my messy hair into a ponytail, shrug into a sweatshirt, and step into shearling boots before leaving my room.

I skip my morning routine and head downstairs because what does a cat care about fresh breath? He sure doesn't have it. And this way, I can pee in my own bathroom instead of the one with the stepstool for Judith. I always trip over that thing.

"Where are you going?" Mom asks from behind me. My hand freezes on the front door handle. She's always been eerily quiet—she could make a career out of sneaking up on people.

"Just down to Gram's," I say without turning around. For some reason, I don't want to see my mom's face—her sadness. "She told me to check up on Junior. I hope I can manage to get him out from under her bed."

"I need to add that to my list," Mom says absentmindedly.

Finally, because it's getting weird, I turn around. She looks . . .
empty. She's fixated on an old water stain on the antique hall
table. "We need to find him a home," she says.

"What?" I ask, surprised. "You can't do that. Gram loved
that cat."

"Don't worry, we'll find someone else who loves him just
as much," Mom says, eyes still on the stain. There's no fire in
her words: She says them like she's programmed to do so.

"I'll take care of him," I protest, staring intently at Mom—
needing her to look at me.

"Albert's allergic to cats. And Judith's afraid of Junior.
He's not living here."

"No, I meant with me at Gram's."

Mom's eyes snap to attention.

"You understand that you're moving back home now that
Gram is gone, right?" she asks. "There's no way I'd let you
live there without parental supervision. And regardless, sell-
ing the house is on my list too."

"You're going to sell the house?" I ask so quietly it's
almost a whisper. Then, a little louder, "How can you even
think about that right now?"

Mom crosses her arms; I know I've hurt her feelings.
"Believe me, I don't want to," she says. "But those were her
final wishes, Caroline. She wanted Teddy to tell me."

Mom looks away, and I imagine that she's thinking about the

fact that she didn't get to say good-bye to her own mother. That, in a way, Gram chose her grandchildren over her daughters.

"Don't stay over there too long," she says in a faraway voice before turning away.

"I won't," I say after her, but she doesn't hear. The door to the kitchen is already swinging back into the hallway.

I jog up the steps to Gram's house and try the door—she always left it unlocked—before realizing what I'm doing. I sigh heavily and walk around to get the key from the magnetic thing under the drainpipe on the side of the house. I go in, lean my back against the door, and take in the house that, for the past five years, has been my home. I look at the brightly painted walls, the dark wood floors. The eclectic furniture. Her handpicked art collection. It's like I can feel the space missing her. I miss her in it.

The sound of my phone makes me jump.

"Hello?" I say quickly, heart pounding.

"Hi," Simone says, and I can tell right off the bat she's using her sympathetic voice today. "How are you *doing*, Linus? Is everything okay? I mean, no, of course it's not okay. But, like, how are you?"

"I'm fine," I say before she continues vomiting words. "Or at least I will be." I hear her sigh on the other end of the line, relieved.

"Sorry for being such a freak," she says. "I just don't really know what to say. . . ."

"There's no right thing," I say. "Honestly, I wish people would just not talk about it right now. I realize that sounds awful, but it's not like I'm not already thinking about her. I only just woke up and it's already too much. I mean last night when we got home, it was just . . . ugh. I wish someone would talk about something else."

"Like what?" Simone asks tentatively.

"Like anything!" I say, finally walking through the entryway and into the house. I weave through the living room and find myself in the kitchen, grabbing a glass and filling it with water like . . . usual. "Tell me about the party last night," I say before drinking half the glass in one gulp.

"For real?" Simone asks, unsure.

"Yes!"

There's a pause when I picture my best friend's internal debate over whether it's selfish or helpful for her to divulge all the juicy details she's dying to share. In the end, her inner gossip wins out. She takes a deep breath, and then, like she's never spoken before and it's some great release to do so, she says everything at once.

"Felicity met some guy in a sweater-vest and he actually danced with her despite the fact that she was wearing those suspenders again—I mean, what is she *thinking*?—and it was geek love by the end of the night. Gwen left early after some girl called her a hooker, which was totally uncalled for, but between you and me, those four-inch heels aren't doing her reputation any favors."

Simone takes a quick breath—only enough so she doesn't pass out but not long enough for me to react—before she dives in again.

"I met a guy named Ed who seemed really great and I know what you're going to say but I'll tell you anyway: I made out with him a little." I can't help it—I laugh.

"You're a professional kisser," I say, thrilled by the normalcy of the conversation. "You kiss guys the second you meet them."

"I do not!" Simone protests, but she laughs, busted.

"You do too," I say. "It's like your version of a handshake. It's a tongue-shake."

"I think I just threw up in my mouth a little," she says. "You're disgusting."

"I speak the truth," I tease.

"Well, you know what they say . . . you have to kiss a lot of frogs to meet your prince," she says good-naturedly. Simone's always known who she is; I love her for that. "And besides, it stops at kissing," she says. "It's not like I'm letting them cop a C-cup on the first date or anything."

"Simone!" I squeal, equally embarrassed by and in love

with her forwardness. "You're so bad," I say, shaking my head. "So, how did it end with Mr. Wonderful Not Wonderful?"

"You really want to know?" she asks in a way that makes me nervous.

"I don't know—do I?"

"Where are you right now?"

"I'm home . . . at Gram's," I say. I can practically hear Simone hesitate—like I just threw a pail of water on her fire—so I quickly add, "Why? Where are you?"

"My house," she says, "but I have an errand to run. I'll pick you up and you can go with me—I'll buy you hot chocolate afterward. Salted caramel hot chocolate."

"That's unfair," I say, drooling like one of those dogs in the science experiment. "Why do I feel like this isn't going to end well?"

"It'll be fine, Linus," she says. "I'm just messing around. The guy gave me his sweatshirt and then texted me this morning, wanting it back. Classic ploy to get to bathe in my awesomeness a little longer," she says, laughing at her own joke. "Anyway, I'm going to drop it off, then we can go hang out. I'm not into the guy—I just want to rip off the Band-Aid and it'll be done. But then I get to see you and give you a big hug and we can talk about . . . whatever."

"You don't want to go alone, do you?"

"Nope."

"Fine. I'll be your breakup buffer. Just so long as you promise not to mention death," I say. "Or funerals. You have to promise not to talk about anything serious whatsoever."

"Done."

"I need like an hour. I have to go find the cat and walk him."

"You know that's completely deranged, don't you?" she asks. Simone walked Junior with me once and we made it one block in fifteen minutes—Junior was crouched low to the cement, terrified the whole time. Eventually I had to pick him up and carry him back like a baby. Or, I guess, like a cat.

"Yeah, but it was Gram's thing," I say quietly. "Anyway, I have to shower. I'm still wearing my pajamas."

"Pajamas are infinitely better than what Felicity leaves the house in on a daily basis," Simone says. "You should just wear those."

"But what if we run into Joel at the coffee shop or something?" I pause, surprised to admit my crush on Joel so easily. Simone gasps.

"Well, aren't we taking off the training wheels? Are you actually ready to go for it with Joel Ryder, Linus? It's not like it's a gazillion years late or anything."

I smile, blushing slightly. "I don't know about *going* for anything. But I think my unspoken admiration doesn't have to be so silent anymore."

"Well," Simone says, "speaking of Joel . . . he was there last night."

"What?" I ask, gripping the phone and suddenly nervous. "Joel was at the party?"

"Yep. I'll tell you all about it when I get there." She kisses the phone and hangs up, leaving me exhilarated and anxious. Just perfect for trying to lure a skittish cat from under a couch.

I coax Junior out with a mangy mouse toy before snapping him into his leash. I walk him up and down the block in the opposite direction from my house. Then I run up the stairs and shower with my own shampoo, not borrowed baby shampoo from Juju, and search my *real* bedroom for clothes that aren't pajamas. It all feels so normal until I walk down the hall and turn the door handle that leads to Gram's room.

I step inside: It smells like lavender, mint, and rose, and the air is still, like it's waiting for something. Waiting for her. Invisible fingertips run up the back of my neck and I shiver even though the heat's on. *She left it on.*

The room is like its own planet, so far away from my own. I walk over and touch the quilt draped at the end of Gram's bed, soft after years of use. I run my fingers along the smooth wooden footboard, then the top of the low dresser.

"I love you, Gram," I say quietly into her space. "If you can hear me, I just want you to know that."

Nothing happens—nothing changes. But it feels like she

heard me anyway. I leave and head downstairs to wait for Simone. For stories of Joel and kissing strangers and hot chocolate. For anything but empty bedrooms with smells that'll fade over time.

For anything but thinking about Gram.

Simone turns down the heater when I jump in the passenger seat of her silver car, then she gives me a hug that lingers longer than usual. When she pulls back, dark brown eyes on mine, I remind her of her promise.

"No serious talk," I say.

She smiles deviously, then, "Did I tell you that this guy Ed kisses like a dog licking himself?" We both totally lose it; there's a point when I actually wish I'd stop laughing because my stomach muscles hurt from overuse. It wasn't the funniest thing she's ever said, but all of the tension of the past week pours out of me. It's healing.

"You have no idea what I'm picturing right now," I say when we're finally over it and on our way.

"Whatever you're picturing, this guy was worse," she says. "Oh, hey! It's my song!" She turns up the radio and Electric Freakshow's latest blasts throughout the car. We both sing along at the top of our lungs, but when it gets to the part I don't know, I take a deep cathartic breath and let it out.

"Thanks for this," I say, looking at her. She's in a tight

pink sweat suit, and her wild hair looks more model than matted. She glances at me, then back at the road.

"You're welcome," she says, navigating onto the highway. "Now grab my phone and check his text from this morning. I need you to read me the address."

I co-pilot us to a neighborhood across town using the Internet GPS that never quite catches up to where we are. "It's 2026," I say as she begins slowly inching down the street.

"Evens are on the left," Simone murmurs as she continues to creep forward. "That's 2020," she says, pointing to a yellow house with black shutters and accelerating a bit more. "2022 . . ." We pass a brick house with trim that needs a paint job. Then she pulls over on the opposite side of the street. "There it is."

I grin at her. "Good luck."

Simone sighs, then turns to grab a boy's sweatshirt wadded up on the backseat. I reach to switch between radio stations.

"I'll be thirty seconds and then it's hot choc-o-latte time," she says before shutting the door and jogging across the street.

In the emptiness of the car, the new station whispers out Electric Freakshow's song again. It's barely loud enough to hear:

". . . are all just magnets for fate; stumbling, skipping, running at our pace . . ."

I whisper along, looking over as Simone takes the front porch steps. She rings the bell, looking back once to give me a thumbs-up, and then talks briefly to a cute guy who doesn't look at all like a dog kisser to me. I guess that's why you really can't judge a book by its cover. She hands over his sweatshirt and gives him an awkward hug. As she jogs back to the car, he watches her go.

"Sammy's?" she asks as she gets behind the wheel.

"Where else?" I ask, my mouth watering again thinking about Sammy's famous salted caramel hot chocolate with a shot of espresso. "I need a scone, too. I haven't eaten anything since . . ." My words fade as I think of the last meal I ate. I need a distraction.

"You didn't tell me about Joel," I say quickly. "At the party?"

"Oh, right!" she says, smacking her leg. "He asked about you."

"Liar!"

"Truth," she says. We're still parked, and I'm sure Ed is wondering why we haven't left yet. Simone goes on. "So Joel was all, 'Where's your sidekick?' and I was all, 'Dealing with family drama,' and he was all, 'Bummer.' And then some girl barfed on the dance floor, which cleared the party faster than a raid."

"I can't believe it," I say, shaking my head.

"Believe it, sister," Simone says, checking her reflection in the rearview. "Your little lover boy might just have eyes for you, too."

I don't say anything else; I just take it all in. Simone shifts gears, and over her shoulder, the hookup house catches my eye. There's a different boy leaving, and from this vantage point he looks even cuter than the first. Blond hair, blue-eyed college random. I nearly smile at him, but Simone peels out like she's driving the getaway car at a bank heist and I almost topple into the backseat.

"Mony!" I yell as I straighten up. She apologizes, and I look back at the house once again. I see the guy stop on the sidewalk, shield his eyes from the sun, and watch after us. There's a flit in my chest that feels like missing something. Then as quickly as he's there—the staring, stirring boy— Simone takes a turn and he's gone.

SIX

GO

I feel like an orphan, even though I'm in my mother's house and my father's called three times already to check up on me. No one's mentioned that I left last night, left Gram, but I can feel it. I can feel it in my mom's silence. My sister's glare. My brother's kindness.

I sit in the bedroom at my mother's house, staring out the window like a caged animal longing for escape. This is exactly how I felt during my parents' divorce. Alone. Scared. When self-preservation mode kicks in, I climb out of bed and dial Simone. It goes to voice mail once again, and anger burns me up—she should know how much I need her now. She should have known how much I needed to stay with my grandmother last night.

I walk over to my closet and pull out the nearest thing to me: a Clinton State University sweatshirt—Teddy's college. Christopher's college.

Suddenly the witty stranger from last night seems like my only friend left in the world. He's obviously not, I know this. But it doesn't stop me from grabbing my backpack and stuffing it full of extra clothes before slipping down the stairs and out the front door.

Chris was right—the houses really do all look different in the daytime. I drive past the old church on the corner as the dim morning light begins to brighten. The street is lined with eccentric houses of blues and yellows that I didn't notice in the dark. Everything is familiar and strange at the same time.

"Damn," I murmur to myself, slowing to creeper-van speed until I pause near the end of the block. The truck is gone that Chris had pointed out before, but the red house halfway down the street looks about right. I pull up to the curb, trying out the space, then decide that's not it.

I do this—up and down the street like a tried-and-true stalker—until my phone buzzes on the passenger seat. I turn frantic when I see it's Simone.

"Where have you been?" I ask. "I've been looking for you since last night." A mixture of anger and relief floods me when I hear her voice.

"I'm so sorry," she says. "I didn't mean to . . . I'm sorry about Gram and for dragging you to that stupid party. God, Linus. Do you hate me?"

"No," I say automatically, but look down at my lap. *I hate myself.* She must still be worried, because she's quiet, and I know I have to fill the void. "I just thought you were canceling our best-friends-forever contract," I mumble.

"Never," she responds with a soft laugh. "It's a blood oath."

There's a pause when neither of us speaks, and I feel . . . different. Like I don't have anything to say. Or rather, that I do. *Why did you make me go?* But I know I can't blame her. Rationally, I know that.

The radio set ends and a commercial comes on; I switch the station and Electric Freakshow's "Magnets for Fate" is playing. I close my eyes as I listen. ". . . sidewalk paved in hitches; broken hearts not fixed by stitches . . ."

"Linus," Simone starts, clearly feeling the void that's opened between us. "Everyone's looking for you. Your mom and Teddy both called me. They're worried. *I'm* worried. You've got to go home."

I shake my head even though she can't see me. "I can't go back there," I murmur into the phone. "I can't face them again. I left. I left my family and I just can't deal with the fallout of that right now."

"You have to," Simone says. "At least for now. The funeral's Tuesday and I will be right there by your side." She pauses. "I screwed up last night, Caroline," she adds quietly.

"I left my phone in the car when I went out later with Felicity and Gwen. I didn't check it until this morning. I was distracted, and I know that makes me a horrible friend. But I'm sorry."

"I'm on my way back," I say. Not, "It's okay, I understand." I can't bring myself to say that. "I'll call you later," I tell her.

Simone is quiet until she mumbles a good-bye. After we hang up, I look around my car, seeing the makings of a bad *Dateline* special on runaways. Where did I think I would go? With Chris—the stranger from last night who could be a serial killer for all I know? And even if he's not, he's a college guy who went to pick up a girl at a party—wham, bam. It's delusional to think he'd really want my brand of drama.

"Dumb," I say, pulling into the street as I start toward home—leaving behind my ideas of escape. At least for now.

Somehow I make it through two more days without taking off again, though admittedly, I spend a lot of it holed up in my room—a room that doesn't feel like home. Finally, Tuesday comes.

In black dresses and suits, the family meets in the entryway and somberly caravans to the church. We sit in the first few pews; Gram's in a casket up front. There's a massive, framed picture of her on an easel to the right, and I stare at it until I think it's moving. Then I look away.

I am numb through the ceremony—Mom has to elbow me when it's my turn to read and I do it like I'm having an out-of-body experience. I feel like I'm watching from miles away when Natalie breaks down during her own reading. I close off my feelings—everything. I watch, unfeeling, as Albert leads Natalie back to her seat.

Afterward, we go to Gram's house, which is catered for a formal after-wake get-together thanks to Aunt Claudia. I loiter in the living room, thinking that Gram would've preferred a casual party to this. When no one's looking, I slip upstairs and spend the rest of the time in my old room. Packing. I don't cry, or rather, I don't *let* myself cry.

Once everyone leaves, my mother and Aunt Claudia steal away to my grandmother's bedroom to sort through her papers—something that feels so violating, I go downstairs and play the TV really loudly. At one point Junior jumps onto my lap and I run my fingers through his white fur like Gram used to.

I watch the television mindlessly until Teddy comes in and drops down on the couch next to me, scaring Junior away. I shoot him a pointed look, and he laughs. "Sorry."

"Doesn't matter," I say. "He doesn't like anyone but Gram anyway."

"Little bastard."

I laugh softly, and then my brother clears his throat like he's about to make a speech. "I've been thinking, Coco," Teddy says. "Maybe you should come back to Clinton with me."

I lift one eyebrow, smiling a little. "Are you going to sneak me into the dorms?"

He shrugs as if it's a possibility, but he doesn't elaborate. Instead he turns back to the television. It's not until five minutes later that I catch on to what he was thinking.

"Dad." I've barely spoken the word out loud when my mother and Aunt Claudia are coming downstairs, arguing over some of the finer points of Gram's estate. I hate hearing them talk about Gram's belongings as if this is a garage sale, so I ask Teddy to walk with me back to Mom's so I can sleep.

We don't say anything about my father on the walk home. I wouldn't even know where to start—I hardly said a word to my dad at the funeral, and he didn't stay long at Gram's house after. But as I lie in bed that night, I think about how much he doesn't know about me anymore—and how in some ways, that's a good thing. If nothing else, at least he won't be disappointed.

I was twelve years old when my parents divorced. It wasn't amicable or well planned. It was like an explosion of feelings—the shrapnel of their anger embedding in all of us. Natalie was only fourteen, but she stuck to Mom like glue. Teddy was sixteen, busy enough with his own life to avoid seeing the drawn-out fights. The hurtful comments.

But I witnessed it all up to the point where I went to my grandmother and begged her to take me in. She spoke to my parents about it. My father protested, and my mother cried, but ultimately Gram strongly suggested that perhaps I'd fare better out of the crosshairs, and they begrudgingly agreed. It was only supposed to be for a little while. When my dad finally moved out three months later, I cut ties with him. I didn't have a good reason. Maybe I felt like, since he was choosing to leave the house, he was choosing to leave me. He still sends a birthday card with twenty bucks in it, and he and Teddy have dinners on Sundays. He and Natalie speak on the phone occasionally. But my father's like a stranger—albeit a polite one.

Which makes considering living with him even more terrifying.

I wake up with the kind of clarity that comes when your sleeping brain resigns itself to something, and I walk downstairs with purpose. My mother and Natalie are at the kitchen table; Albert's probably at work, and my guess is that my oldest and youngest siblings are still asleep. The house is silent even with Mom and Natalie together, like they're communicating telepathically—noiselessly hating me. The house is still, but in the morning after the funeral, there is no peace. It's just emptiness.

I swallow hard as I sit across from my mother, staring at

her until she looks up. When she does, she seems startled, as if I appeared out of nowhere.

"Caroline," she says. "Did you want breakfast?"

I knot my hands together under the table, wondering whether the words will be able to pass my lips. "I want to go live with Dad," I say quietly. My sister gasps, but I'm only courageous enough to dart a quick look at her expression. I can't believe I just said that out loud.

"W-what?" my mother stammers. "Why?"

"I . . . can't stay here anymore, Mom." My voice cracks over her name. "It just hurts too much." But I know Gram isn't the only reason I'm leaving: I can't handle being the odd man out in my own family.

Natalie shakes her head, her mouth open in disbelief. "You think the rest of us don't miss Gram just as much as you do?" she asks. "Do you think you're so damn special that you deserve a reset button whenever life gets tough?"

"I know I'm not special," I say, matching my sister's tone. Hot tears race down my cheeks, and I grip the edge of the table so I don't lose my resolve. "And I know exactly what you think of me." I dart a pleading look at my mother. "Just give me a chance to rebuild," I say. "Please, Mom. I can't deal here. I'm falling apart."

She runs her hand roughly through her hair, leaning closer to me. "But if we're together—"

"I don't want to be together," I say. "I want to be alone—or at least be able to start fresh. I want to be someone else. And I can do that at Dad's house."

My sister pushes back from the chair and jumps up. "That won't make it better, Caroline. Do you think Dad won't see what a jerk you are?"

"Natalie," my mother says quietly, touching my sister's arm.

"No, Mom," she says, and then points at me. "You're a runner, Caroline. You run away from everything and everyone at the first sign of trouble. And you don't care who you leave behind." Her contempt for me is obvious—it's pushing me harder out the door. *Why can't she ever just back down?*

"Think of someone else for a change," Natalie adds, then, quieter, "Think of *Mom*."

I turn my gaze to my mother, but she can't look at me. The coldness of that—of my mother too distraught to even look at me—makes what I say next even more disgusting.

"Let me go, Mom. Let me start over."

My mother is trembling as she picks up a spoon to stir her coffee, not looking up. "I'll call your father this afternoon," she says calmly. My sister stalks away with a sort of hatred I choose not to acknowledge.

"I'm sorry," I say so softly to my mother that I'm not sure she hears me. I stay seated for the most awkward minute of my life, deafened by silence, before I leave to go back upstairs. The entire way to my room I think that I can't stop disappointing them.

Even now I see that my every move just compounds the hurt I caused when I was twelve. I don't think I can make it better, ever make it better. But without Gram I'm lost. I can't bring her back, but I'm not sure I can live with her gone either. Mostly, though, I'm just terrified that my sister is right about me.

SEVEN

STAY

"You didn't tell me you were coming back to school today," Simone says, elbowing the guy with the locker next to mine as she wiggles her curves into my personal space. Simone studies me with her black-lined eyes, managing to look both concerned and—probably because I didn't tell her this one little piece of information—annoyed at the same time.

"The service was yesterday," I say. "I'm back." I pull books from my bag—books I took home Friday but never cracked open—and shove them into the messy metal box. It's Wednesday, my grandmother died five days ago, and for the first time in my life, I don't give a crap about school.

"I know, dummy, I was there," my friend says softly. "I just thought you'd take a few more days off. At least the rest of the week."

"For what? To stare at Natalie?" I say, pulling my English book from the teetering tower of junk.

"Yeah, *that's* not a good idea," she says.

"Actually, I didn't mean it like that," I say. "It's weird, but this whole thing has sort of nixed the drama in my house. It's like we're all in the same boat now. Bonded by misery."

"For serious?" Simone asks, looking surprised.

"I mean at least for now," I say. "Who knows what'll happen later. But my mom keeps wanting to just hang out and look at pictures and watch movies and eat ice cream. It's just . . ."

"Too much," Simone finishes my sentence. "I totally get that. People deal in different ways."

"Right," I say. "To me, looking at those pictures just makes it worse. It's not going to bring her back. Either way, Gram's gone."

"I know, Linus, I . . ." Simone's expression is filled with pity; I look away and slam my locker door shut. "I'm sorry," she says, hugging me. I don't reciprocate—not because I don't want to, but because my reaction time's too slow. Something about being back at school where everything is normal reminds me more of Gram and how abnormal my life is right now.

"Walk you to English?" she offers.

I turn from my locker and weave into the flow of traffic; Simone falls in step with me and out of nowhere, Gwen and Felicity appear behind us like fighter pilots in formation. The hall is jam-packed because there are only five minutes before first period—everyone is either doing last-minute book swaps or trying to get in a few more seconds of gossip before the mandatory no texting time starts. I can hear nails on smart screens behind me the entire way down the long, main hallway. We turn into the English corridor; at the door to Mrs. Martin's room, Simone gives me a side squeeze.

"It'll get better," she says quietly. Sincerely.

"Thanks," I say automatically. I still haven't cried since Gram died, and it's starting to really bother me. Yesterday Natalie said she thinks I might be in shock.

"In the meantime, at least you have *that* to look at all period," she says, lifting a chin toward the classroom door. Joel is walking through it; my stomach flips over.

"At least there's that," I say, smiling.

"Love you, chick," Simone says quickly before turning and walking away with two texting shadows trailing behind her. Before they turn the corner, Gwen looks back and catches my attention. Baring midriff in October and teetering on too-high heels, phone still in her hand, she blows me a kiss. It's not a flirty, silly one; instead it's a kiss that I can almost see floating through the air and landing softly on my cheek like the brush of a butterfly wing. I smile sadly at her before she disappears into the throngs of students. Then I head into class, feeling a teeny bit better from the unexpected show of kindness.

Joel's scribbling intently in his notebook as I take my seat three rows over and two seats back. His hair is freshly cut short—he must have chopped it this weekend. He's wearing a black Electric Freakshow T-shirt, the jeans he wears most often, and my favorite pair of his seemingly endless supply of Converse. I can see his wallet chain dangling down from his chair. I might be the freak show myself, but I've always wanted to grab him by it.

I'm still staring at Joel when, without warning, he looks right at me. His eyes are dark brown up close but from far away, they look black. They match his hair and eyelashes and the stubble that grows on his chin every so often when he doesn't feel like shaving. He smiles at me, sympathetic.

"You okay?" he mouths. Even if class wasn't starting, I doubt he would've said it aloud. Joel doesn't like drawing attention to himself. Too bad his looks make that an impossible task.

I nod, then mouth back, "Thanks."

Joel refocuses on his work and I try to slow my heart, feeling like a child for getting so amped up every time he even *looks* at me. I mean, it's not like I haven't been around him forever.

Joel and I met at the community swimming pool the summer before fourth grade. I'd gone to private school before then, but my parents transferred me to public when we moved across town. I didn't know anyone in my neighborhood, and that summer I did a lot of swimming alone. I thought it was going to be the state of things until one day Joel set up camp on the lounge chair next to mine. Unlike the other boys, he was T-shirted and dry; he preferred comics to human cannonballs. He was a lot skinnier then.

There was no memorable introduction; in fact, Joel didn't speak at all. He just sat next to me . . . that day and the next and the next. Soon enough, if one of us went to the snack bar, we brought back two Popsicles. Eventually we did have conversations—his focused mostly on Spider-Man while mine were mainly about bubble gum lip gloss—and when school started, even though he didn't choose the desk next to mine, I felt more confident when he was around. It's not like we hung out after that—Simone spun me into her web on the first day and never let me out—but I've always felt a connection.

There was a moment when I thought he felt it too—at a party two summers ago. I'd been sure he was going to make a move. But he didn't, and we remained the kind of friends who are comfortable hanging out together but don't do so on purpose.

Distracted by thoughts of Joel, I feel class fly by; soon enough the bell's ringing and everyone's gone and I'm working my way through the rest of the day. After the emotional bump of seeing the guy I like, I'm back to zombie for the remainder of the morning, with movements and sights and sounds sort of just blurring together and drifting by. Between classes I send Simone a text to tell her I'm stopping by home for lunch. It's a lie—really, I just want to be alone.

At my locker I toss in my bag, then remove my wallet and car keys even though I have no idea where I'm going. I turn toward the main exit—the one that'll take me through the commons and therefore past . . . everyone. Instead of walking, I flip around toward the auditorium, thinking I'll use the back exit and go around the side of the building. But when I walk by the open auditorium doors, I find myself going in.

The auditorium is cool and dark, with only a couple of lights eerily illuminating the stage up ahead. It smells like cleaning solution and cookies, which strikes me as odd until I remember that Family Sciences is in this wing. I half-walk, half-stumble down the carpeted middle aisle and take a seat in a creaky, cushioned chair in the orchestra section. I'm like the only person at a badly reviewed musical on opening night, waiting for something to happen. Then something does.

"Hiding from someone?" a guy's voice says.

It can't be.

I turn. Joel is standing in the aisle behind me.

"Everyone," I admit, managing to appear calm despite my

complete shock that he's here. "I don't feel much like facing the masses today."

"Should I leave?" he asks, no emotion in his eyes. That's the killer thing about Joel: His expressions give nothing away. He doesn't move, waiting for my response.

"No, stay," I say quickly. I move over one seat, motioning for him to sit. "What are you doing here?" I ask.

"I saw you come in." He sits and shifts to get comfortable, like it's nothing. "I was curious."

"Oh."

We both stare straight ahead at the stage, like we're watching a performance silent and invisible to the outside world. "I love this part," I joke, hoping to lighten the mood. Saturday with Simone was so great—I want to replicate that lack of seriousness now. But Joel just looks at me funny. "You know, when the dancers leap into the air like that," I say, pointing to the empty stage.

"Funny," he says, but he doesn't laugh. And he doesn't keep the made-up story going either. Instead, his eyes still on the ballet that isn't there, he floors me by opening up. "My uncle died last year," he says, matter-of-fact. "I'm not sure if you remember, but my dad left when I was a kid. . . ."

I remember.

"My uncle sort of stepped in," he continues. "We were thick."

"That's kind of how it was with me and my gram," I say. "I went to live with her when my parents were going through their bloodbath divorce."

"Yeah," Joel says, shifting in his chair. His muscular legs are so long that he looks uncomfortable in the seat. "My uncle used to take me to baseball games in the city. He paid for art classes. He was solid."

"What happened?" I ask quietly. "I mean, if you're okay with telling me. You don't have t—"

"Hunting accident," he cuts in. "He was out with friends and they were drinking. They were dicking around, not paying attention. Long story short, he got shot."

"Oh my God," I whisper. "I'm so sorry." *How did I not know about this? Why are you so secretive?*

An awkward amount of time passes, and just when I think he might stand and leave, Joel turns and looks at me. "Death sucks." He stares with brown-black eyes like he's branding me. And then, before I have time to consider what's happening, his lips are on mine.

I'm surprised but, oddly, not shocked. Instinctively, maybe because of all the years I've craved him, I kiss back. His lips are strong but soft, and this close, the smell of him is hypnotic. His hand moves up my arm and stops at the base of my skull, under my hair. It sort of pins one side of my body down against the seat, in a good way. My free hand finds his face: It's the beginnings of scruffy. We kiss, long and open mouthed, like we've done it a billion times before. But it's new, and despite the kisses I've shared with boyfriends past, this is the best.

This feels like the first.

Suddenly Joel pulls back, hand still holding my neck, looking a little surprised that he kissed me. There are dozens of words running through my brain—*shock, sorry, yes, wow, again, elation, please, run, hide, more*—but he says none of them. He stares, and I wonder if he thinks I can hear his thoughts. *I wish.*

"I have to go," he says finally, which is not at all what I was expecting. The lunch period doesn't end for another twenty minutes at least. Probably seeing the disappointment on my face, he adds an explanation. "I'm supposed to call Lauren."

My stomach drops: *Did he seriously just say that?* Joel releases his grip on my neck, and the coolness of his hand's absence makes me shiver. He steps into the aisle, looking even more beautiful than he did earlier, if that's possible. Maybe it's because now I know what he tastes like.

"Hey, I didn't mean to . . . ," he begins, his voice trailing off.

"No problem," I say, unsure what I'm forgiving him for but trying to sound lighter than I feel. "It's fine. Go call Lauren." *Did I seriously just say that?* "I'll see you around."

Joel turns to head up the aisle, then hesitates. "Caroline?"

"What?" I ask, and maybe it comes out a little snippy.

"I didn't come in here to—"

"Don't worry about it," I interrupt, because that's what you say. But I know I'm going to be worrying about it for the rest of my natural life. "It was just . . . something that happened. Let's forget all about it."

"That's not what I meant," he says, shaking his head.

"Hey, Joel?" I say, desperately wanting this uncomfortable situation to be over. He looks at me expectantly, like I'm going to have the answer. To say the right thing. Instead, forcefully, I say, "Go call Lauren."

He holds my gaze a moment longer, then finally he nods once and moves up the aisle. I don't turn around to watch him leave, but I hear him close the door behind him. Maybe he knows that I need the space to myself even more now. Or maybe closing the door was just something he did automatically, without thinking for even a fraction of a second about the consequences of doing so.

SEVEN

GO

I stand in the driveway of my father's two-story house, staring up at the white siding, the black shutters. He moved in here a few months ago with his new wife, Debra, but I've never visited. And now I'm moving in.

I look doubtfully at my brother as he comes up the driveway with one of my suitcases. He told me on the way over that Dad and Debra are trying to have a baby. They probably didn't expect her to be a teenager. When my brother sees my expression, he shakes his head.

"Don't be judgey," Teddy says. "I know you don't want to like Deb, but she's really nice."

"And closer to your age." I look sideways at him, and he laughs.

"She's thirty, Coco. Not twenty. And she teaches anthropology at Clinton, so don't try to outsmart her. She'll be onto you." He elbows my side before leading me across the walkway.

As I get to the door, my heart pounds with an uncertainty I haven't felt in years. Not since I waited on Gram's porch that day. This time I let my mother handle the details, and she and my father had a long talk about my future—even if she made it clear my stay here would only be temporary. She called my current state of mind a "phase." I couldn't bring myself to pick up the phone and talk to my dad; I didn't know what to say. Now I'm regretting it. I feel like a foreign exchange student coming to live with a new host family.

I take one last look at the street behind me and then ring the doorbell. Teddy kicks my foot lightly, reminding me that I'm not alone in this. But he'll be back at his dorm tonight while I'll be sleeping in the house of a practical stranger who my father happens to be married to. And is trying to have a baby with. Gross.

The door opens and there's my dad, with his dark hair graying at the temples, wearing a warm smile and a sweater too heavy for being inside. He looks the same as always except maybe, if I'm honest, happier.

"Hi, guys," he says in the voice that used to read me *Goodnight Moon*. He and Teddy do one of those back-smacking hugs, both of them beaming. I watch, smiling politely. When Dad's eyes fall on mine, I see relief. He reaches out and pulls me into his arms.

I stand there, awkwardly, until I pat him on the back. "Thanks for this, Dad," I say. "I really appreciate it."

He nods and I think he's afraid his voice will crack if he talks, so he soundlessly waves me and my brother inside. Teddy takes my things upstairs as I follow my father, getting the first look at his house. It's weird—there are pieces of furniture from my childhood strewn about an entirely new home. The leather recliner, the painting of the Italian villa over the fireplace.

And to my surprise, there's a picture of Gram along with other family photos hanging on the wall near the dining room table. I spin back to my father. "Where's Debra?" I ask.

"She has classes today, but she wanted to be here to welcome you. She's making a special dinner tonight." He looks so hopeful.

"I, uh . . . I told Teddy I'd go with him to his dorms to hang out for a little bit. Is . . . that okay?" It feels strange to ask his permission to go out.

"Oh. Yeah, of course. Here, let me show you around first."

My father seems a little bummed that I'm not going to eat Debra's dinner, but still he's lively as he gives me the tour of the house. Even though I'm only thirty minutes away from where I used to live, the entire vibe is different. We walk from the living room double doors to the backyard, which is tree-lined and covered with bright orange and yellow leaves. The kitchen is big and airy, and there's a dark den that reminds me of old dudes smoking cigars. I decide after having only seen the main level that although my father's house is a mansion to me, it still manages to feel homey.

On the way to the second floor, my dad tells me about my new school—which I'll start on Monday. For a second, I'm surprised at the idea. But then I remind myself that I'm not at sleepaway camp. I've changed my life. I'm not exactly sure how I feel about that yet.

"This is your room," he says, sounding both excited and afraid.

He pushes open the door, and immediately I smile. There isn't a penguin in sight. The walls are a soft brown, the curtains luxurious with long panels of red and gold. My bed is a queen, overflowing with decorator pillows and satiny sheets. This is a grown-up room, and I'm absolutely beside myself at how perfect it is.

"You like it," he says, laughing at his own relief.

"I love it," I correct. I turn to my dad and almost hug him, stopping myself just before. But he must have read my thought because he reaches to put his palm on my shoulder and smiles.

"I'm so glad, Caroline. And Debra will be too. She did this for you. She wants you to be happy here."

I nod, not sure how I feel about Debra yet, either. Then I walk into the room, taking a moment to touch all the fabrics and test out the bed. After the third bounce on the mattress, I look up to see my dad loitering in the hall. I guess he's just as unsure about this entire situation as I am.

"I'm going to settle in," I tell him. "Before I go over to Teddy's."

"Right," my father says. "Yes. I'll see you later, then." He waves, but just as he's about to leave, he glances back at me. "I'm glad you're here, honey. I really am."

He's genuine; I know he is. I smile and thank him politely, wishing I had the guts to say it back. The second he's gone, I don't waste any time before closing the door and whipping out my phone to call Simone. I hesitate, thinking back on that day at the hospice—the day I left. *It wasn't her fault,* I think. *She's my best friend, and it wasn't her fault.* I dial her number.

Simone's quiet when she answers. "How is it?" she asks.

"Weird," I say, trying to make us normal again. "Things are weird all over, Mony."

"Weird like you not calling me anymore?" she asks in a shaky voice. "Or weird like you uprooting your entire life— my entire life—without so much as asking what I thought? Did you wonder how I'd feel about you moving away? Did you even care?"

I didn't. When I made the decision to leave, I didn't take Simone into consideration. But I'm tired of feeling guilty. I'm tired of feeling anything.

"It's only thirty minutes," I tell her, but know the excuse is flat.

"Thirty minutes," she repeats with the correct amount of emphasis. "That means a half-hour difference every lunch period, every trip to the mall. I know things suck for you right now; I get it. But I think you're being a coward." The word hits me hard, making my eyes tear up.

"I shouldn't have left with you that night," I say quietly. It's my only comeback, even if it's an unfair one. To drive home that point, Simone gets really quiet—extending the silence long enough for me to wonder if she's still there. But then she sniffles.

"Go ahead, Linus," she says. "Blame me. Blame your sister. Hell, blame everyone. Just make sure you don't take any responsibility for yourself. That would be too harsh."

I narrow my eyes, anger starting to seep into my tone. "Oh, I hate myself just plenty," I say. "But thanks for reminding me how much I suck. Look, I have to go. I'll call you later."

"Yeah, sure. If you can fit me into your schedule, I'll be around." And then she hangs up without saying good-bye.

I set my phone on the bed next to me and focus on trying to quiet the desperation that comes with fighting with your best friend. I hate her just a little, even though I know I really hate myself. I need to pull it together before I can go back downstairs. I calm my heart, steady my breathing.

I change into a worn T-shirt and soft jeans, opting for lip balm instead of any real sort of makeup. Hanging out with Teddy will set me right—it always has before. For a minute, I'm actually looking forward to seeing the campus again, to being around other people. I'm going somewhere where I can feel comfortable. My dad's house doesn't inspire that feeling. At least not yet.

Teddy calls up that he has to leave, and I pause to take in my reflection one last time before going downstairs. I look worn and broken. I look like a tattered version of me.

"Runner," I whisper accusingly, watching the reflection as her eyes fill with tears. And as the first one trickles down her cheek, I watch her brush it away and walk out the door.

The town of Clinton is quiet and kempt as I leave my father's house, following my brother's car. Little patters of rain begin to hit my windshield, and I glance uncertainly at the sky, wondering what's to come.

Luckily the dorms are only fifteen minutes away from my dad's because what started as a sprinkle turns into a torrential downpour as we pull into the parking lot. My brother snags the last spot in the main lot and then runs to my window and directs me toward the visitors' lot—otherwise known as Siberia.

I pull up the hood of my jacket and jog—trying, and failing, to avoid the puddles. When I get to Teddy, safely waiting under the entrance overhang, I take a second to look over the campus. The trees, the brick of the buildings, even the crooked stop sign are the same. Gram loved coming here. Her excitement when visiting Teddy was always infectious. She once told me it made her feel young to be around young people. Then she'd lick her palm and smooth down one of the stray hairs in my part. I nearly drown in the grief of the memory, how much I took her love for granted.

"Hey," my brother says, bumping me. "It's okay to miss her, you know. You don't always have to keep a brave face." He's like a mind reader.

I lower my head. "Do you hate me for leaving that night?"

Teddy gasps and puts his arm over my shoulders to pull me into a sideways hug. "Of course not, Coco. And neither would Gram. You don't seriously think that, do you?"

Yes. "Not really," I say instead, not wanting to drag him into my grief and guilt. "I just . . ." I pull back to look into Teddy's worried eyes. "I wish I was as strong as you."

His expression weakens. "I'm not nearly as pulled together as you think. Listen," he says quietly. "Gram would want us to be together. All of us. So this thing with Natalie, with Mom— it's got to end, Coco." He smiles a little. "Even if I'm glad to have you close by."

"I'm glad too." And I mean it. Being here with Teddy—it helps. And even though I can't imagine a world where Natalie and I don't hate each other, I think that my brother is right. Gram would want us all together. Unfortunately, I don't think it'll ever happen. "So . . . ," I tell my brother, putting my chilled hands in the pockets of my hoodie. "Are we going inside or do you want to continue this heart-to-heart while I freeze to death?"

Teddy laughs. "Inside," he says, pulling open the door. "But I'm ordering pizza before any more talking. You made me miss Debbie's roast."

I smile, walking past him through the door. The dorm lobby is a dirty white with army-green lockers lining the walls, posters for upcoming events taped and retaped to pillars. The elevator is slow and loud, and I have to remind myself each time I ride in it that it won't get stuck—mostly to keep from panicking.

The floor is silent as we head toward his room. Teddy has a double with his best friend from high school, Phillip Voss, who I've known since I was a kid. Phillip pegs me in the face with a dirty sock the minute I walk in, and suddenly everything is so normal I actually laugh. I pick up the sock, ready to throw it back, but then I realize it's a *dirty sock* and drop it.

"Wimp," Phillip calls, and goes back to watching *The Simpsons*. Teddy calls in the pizza as I shrug out of my jacket and take up space on the saggy beanbag.

Teddy's room hasn't changed since he moved in—posters

everywhere, especially Electric Freakshow, and a few over Phillip's bunk that he refers to as his "girlfriends." Sure, if he happened to be dating a pinup model in a swimsuit.

When the pizza arrives, the three of us pounce, calling dibs on the biggest slices and then groaning when someone else takes them. But once our mouths are too full to talk, we finish watching *The Simpsons* and relax into the comfort of college life.

After his third slice, Phillip decides to share some of his favorite dorm stories, to which I half-listen and half-cringe.

"You could see her black G-string through her white sweats," he says, shaking his head. "And I'm pretty sure she did it on purpose."

"Phillip, you're disgusting," I respond, biting into my slice while still staring at the television. "I can't believe any girl would go out with you." Phil isn't entirely revolting. It's just that he crossed into that annoying-brother status years ago.

And then he smacks me on the back of the head with a pillow. The room erupts into laughter. There are a few more hits until Teddy has to break it up before we really start to throw down. When it's done, we all sigh.

"I've missed you, snot nose," Phillip says fondly from above me on the futon.

"You too, reject." I glance at the clock on Teddy's dresser and see that it's nearly ten. I'm not sure if I have a curfew, but it seems wrong to stay out until midnight on my first night at Dad's. I tell Teddy and Phillip good night and make my brother promise to come over for a "family" dinner tomorrow. I tell him I'll need moral support.

As I cross the lobby of the dorm, I pause to fold the still-wet cuff of my jeans where they slip under the heels of my sneaker. I do a quick hop, trying to steady my balance. A cold rush of air hits me as the door opens, and when I look up, I suck in a startled breath. And nearly tumble to the floor.

Chris lifts his head, his mouth opening with surprise. But rather than ask what I'm doing here, he smiles. "This totally counts as one of those random times," he says, and takes out his phone.

I laugh, not sure how to respond. More than anything, I'm pretty stunned to have *actually* bumped into him again.

"Well?" he asks. "I believe your exact phrase was that I could have *the digits*. So hand them over, Sweet Caroline."

"Don't sing it."

"I never will." He pauses. "Okay, I might once or twice. But I will try to control any musical outbursts." When I still don't give him my number, Chris slides his phone back into his pocket and walks to lean against the wall of mailboxes. "Can I at least assume you were stalking me?" he asks hopefully.

"Not this time." When he glances away, I take the opportunity to size him up. He's wearing a black thermal with no coat, and his arms are more muscular than I had noticed at the party. His blond hair is messy, but sort of adorable in its own way. His eyes are a shade of blue you only see in the sky on the clearest day. Maybe it's the buzz of a normal night at last, or maybe I'm intrigued, but I go to rest against the mailboxes next to Chris.

"I regretted not giving you my number," I say, staring at my sneakers. "The day after my gram died was horrible. I tried to find you, but"—I look sideways at him—"you're right. The houses do look different in the daylight."

A broad smile crosses his face. "It was the red one."

I snap my fingers at the missed opportunity, and then we go back to leaning silently, even as more students enter the building. After a minute he pulls out his phone, the screen lit up before he hits ignore. I start to fidget.

"So what floor do you live on?" I ask. "My brother's on six."

Chris seems surprised. "Oh, I don't live here. I'm just stopping by to see a friend. That's who keeps calling, actually."

I laugh. "So you're the ditcher this time?"

"She'll get over it," he says with a shrug. I feel a pinch of jealousy.

"Your girlfriend?" I ask, trying to sound casual. Chris pulls his eyebrows together.

"Do you think I'd be asking for your phone number if I had a girlfriend? Wow, you really do think I'm a douche."

"No, I—"

"Just a friend," he says. "Maria is a friend and I actually have several others, all of which I'd ditch for a short amount of time if you'd agree to go get coffee with me. Right now."

"I can't."

Chris nods, then takes his phone out again. "God," he says, hitting ignore. But before he can put it away, I take it from his hand.

I can feel his stare on the side of my face as I click into his contacts and enter my number. When I type in my name, I put Sweet Caroline. He watches me do all of this without a word, and when I'm done, his bright blue eyes find mine.

"I'll call you," he says with a victorious grin.

"Maybe soon?" I ask, feeling like I should hug him or somehow acknowledge that I'm completely and totally flirting back.

"Oh, it'll be soon," he says. "I'm not letting you slip away this time. Even if you run."

The word "run" sends a shiver over me, but I refuse to let even one bad thought in right now.

"It's still raining," Chris says as he slowly backs away. "So drive safely. The bridge is out on Brinkerhoff if you're going that way."

"I'm not. My dad lives really close, but thanks for the warning."

Chris walks to the elevator, looking back as if debating whether or not to stay longer, but when it opens, he just smiles and gets in.

And I'm not even to my car when a text pops up on my phone.

TOTALLY LIKE FATE.

EIGHT

STAY

After school, I feel like I'm a bubble on the verge of being popped, only I'm not as afraid of spilling air as I am of spilling emotions. Reeling from the kiss with Joel and overrun with sadness about Gram, I know I need to keep myself busy—my thoughts at bay. So I head to my room hell-bent on dismantling Penguin Palace.

He followed me into the auditorium. I stuff my penguin sheets into a trash bag. *He confided in me about his uncle. Why now?* Down go the kid posters from the walls. Juju gets the lovely penguin snow globe that Dad brought back from his honeymoon in New Zealand. *What was with the kiss?* Bye-bye, hideous lamp. Mom can deal with that one. *He's an amazing kisser—even better than I imagined.* I smooth down the black-and-white comforter that Gram gave me. *Gram can probably hear me thinking about kissing boys. Boys with girlfriends.*

My cell rings, making me jump. I go over and check the caller ID—I can't believe what it says. Last year during Simone's *The Secret* phase, she had me program Joel's number into my phone—a way of telling the universe to make him call. He never did. Um, until now.

"Joel?" I say like a complete loser, as if I've been waiting by the phone for him. I'd smack myself if I didn't think he might be able to hear it.

"Hi, Caroline," he says with that voice of his—that quiet, commanding voice that's never light, no matter the situation. "Is this . . . are you busy?"

"I'm not, actually," I say, sitting down on my pristine bed. "I just finished doing . . . something."

"What were you doing?" he asks.

"I was just fixing my room—at my mom's," I say. "I had to move back after, you know." I look around, amazed by how much more "me" I feel now that I have my own stuff.

"Got it," he says. We're both quiet for a few seconds, then, "So listen, I wanted to call and apologize for today."

"Really, it's fine," I say quickly, not wanting to talk about it.

"No, seriously, I feel like a dick for kissing you—like I took advantage of you when you were upset or something. I mean, I've known that you liked me for a while but—"

"What?" I interrupt, instantly humiliated by both the

fact that he knows and the fact that he just went ahead and acknowledged it out loud.

"What?"

"What did you just say?" I don't really want to hear it again, but it's like sticking your tongue in a mouth sore—I ask anyway.

"Come on, Caroline," he says quietly. Intimately. "I mean, I'm not wrong, am I?"

I hold my breath, hoping he'll say something else, anything else. But he's silent—waiting for me to answer. "I don't know what you want me to say here, Joel," I tell him. "I mean, so what? We've known each other forever and nothing's ever . . ." I can't say it; I try again. "And you're with Lauren."

"Maybe not for long."

My stomach flips, but I manage not to squeal "REALLY??" into the phone.

"The whole long-distance thing isn't working too well," he says, sighing.

Long distance? She only goes to school across town!

"That's too bad," I say, pretending to be sympathetic. He laughs halfheartedly, calling me on the failed attempt without saying anything.

"She's jealous. You know she got into Clinton but stayed at the community college to be closer to me, right? And she always wants me to call and check in; she wants to know where

I am all the time. She asks me about girls in my classes and who I talk to on a daily basis. . . . It's like she went to college and went batshit."

It's my turn to laugh, but I try to contain it.

"Shouldn't you be the jealous one?" I ask, hating that I'm having a conversation with Joel about his incredibly hot girl-friend. "She's the one surrounded by older guys."

"Jealousy isn't my thing," he says flatly. It sort of bugs me for a reason I can't pinpoint. What do I care if Joel doesn't get jealous? He's not *my* boyfriend. And besides, isn't trusting someone a good thing?

He sighs again. "I don't want to talk about Lauren." *Thank God.* "I was calling to apologize, but also . . . I wanted to tell you that it wasn't just out of the blue for me either. It wasn't like I was trying to get some from the girl in crisis."

"Oh, yeah, I'm *totally* the girl in crisis," I say sarcastically.

"You get what I mean," Joel says, maybe a twinge annoyed.

"Do I?"

"Your grandmother just died—you're not exactly up," he says. The banter is starting to feel a little like a battle.

We're both quiet again, and I'm wondering what excuse he's going to use to get off the phone because clearly this call is not going smoothly.

"You said you're at your house?" he says instead.

"Yes," I answer curiously. "Why?"

"I'm coming to get you." He offers me no choice. "I want to talk to you, but I hate phones. I hate not being able to see your face. I can't tell if you're pissed or mellow or whatever. Let's just go somewhere and hang out for a bit, okay?"

I can't believe what I'm hearing. I look at myself in the mirror by the closet to verify that I look as shocked as I feel. It's worse.

"Okay," I say.

"Fifteen minutes?" he asks. I nod.

"I'll be waiting."

Joel drives a white, vintage Volvo wagon that would look good on no one but a guy completely comfortable in his own skin. I'm sitting on the stoop when he pulls up; he nods at me but doesn't get out. I walk over and climb into the passenger seat; it smells like fake pine, soap, and the faintest hint of cigarettes.

"Do you smoke?" I ask, fastening my seat belt.

"You smell it too? My mom says I'm crazy—she has the worst sense of smell of anyone I know. Anyway, no, I don't smoke—the previous owner did," he says, shaking his head. "This was my uncle's car. The one I told you about? I can't get the smell out. I've used my own cash to have it detailed twice."

"It's not that bad," I say. "You can barely notice it over the air freshener." I bat the tree hanging from the rearview mirror, then feel idiotic for doing it; I shove my hands under my legs to keep them contained. Joel reads it as me being cold and turns up the heat.

"So, where are we going?" I ask as he pulls away from the curb.

"Fairgrounds?" he asks, and in a flash I'm nervous. People go to the fairgrounds to drink or make out—at least that's what Simone tells me. I've only been there once and it was pretty lame.

"Sure," I say, sitting back into the seat and trying to breathe away my anxiety. Joel and I don't talk much the rest of the way, and I wonder whether he and Lauren usually drive in silence or whether they have an infinite number of things to talk about. I can't help but feel like I'm doing it wrong.

Joel takes a right at Magnolia, then pulls through deserted gates with unmanned pay stations that make me think of a scene from a dystopian novel I read last summer. There's a wide expanse of pavement ahead of us: a massive, cracked lot with no streetlights or guidelines. Around the perimeter is a jumpable white fence; to the right is the underside of a grandstand where concerts happen when the fair comes to town. Joel turns in that direction, driving diagonally across the lot and parking expertly between the break in the grandstand so people driving by on Magnolia can't see his car.

"Come on," he says, killing the engine. He opens his door,

so I open mine; now I'm genuinely cold and shivering from the chill. My sweatshirt wasn't a good choice.

"I have an extra jacket in the back—you want it?" he asks.

"Sure."

Joel opens the back door and grabs the fleece-lined denim jacket he wears all the time. I walk around the car and take it from him, then shrug into it, trying not to blow a fuse from the perfect smell of him enveloping me. I want to live and die in this jacket. "Thanks," I manage. "Much better."

I follow Joel through a tunnel and up a ramp to the front of the grandstand, then watch him jump a waist-high chain like it's nothing. I duck and go under, trying not to fall or get my hair caught in the links. He tromps up the metal stairs to the highest possible point, then turns and sits on a cold bench—I trail behind and do the same. Only then do I realize what a great view of the city we have from up here—this side is taller than the one facing us, so we can see the hills to the left and the water to the right.

"This is pretty awesome," I say, leaning back against the wall where one of the luxury boxes is. "I've never been up here."

"I come here a lot to draw," Joel says. "It's peaceful."

"That it is," I say. "And freezing." I shiver and he scoots a little closer to me. He leans back too, and we both stare straight ahead.

"So," he says.

"So."

"Are you mad at me?" he asks. I look at him, surprised.

I decide to make light of the situation, hoping it will help. "Why would I be mad?" I ask. "It's not like I wasn't a participant in the whole auditorium kissing session." But when Joel looks at me with those too-dark eyes, all lightness flies out the window. "I know you have a girlfriend," I say. "I'm not expecting anything."

"But what if I want you to expect something?" he says, holding me like shackles with his gaze. A breeze blows my hair into my mouth, and as I pull it out, I let myself smile.

"Why now?" I ask.

He shrugs—I'm not sure it's the right reaction, but it's all I've got from him. Then, "Maybe it's always been there; I don't know. All I can say is that when things started going to shit with Lauren, you're the one I started thinking about."

"Are you serious?" I ask. I think my heart's going to leap right out of my chest.

"I'm serious," he says. "And this whole thing with your grandma—it's bringing back all those feelings I had for my uncle. I feel like you're the only one who gets me right now."

I'm aware that Joel's words are not quite perfect, but I'm not sure what perfect looks like, either. So when he kisses me again, long and without holding back, I go with it. I feel it deep inside like I want to crush him with all of the emotion surging through my veins, but then he pulls back to have me rest against him and we watch the sunset without speaking.

I think of perfection, and whether it exists.

I think of Lauren, and what she'd be saying or doing were she here instead of me right now. I wonder if Joel is going to break up with her, and whether I'd still come here if he told me he wasn't. I realize that I would.

Then because it's what I do, I think of Gram. This time I don't think about how much I miss her. I don't replay her final words in my mind. Instead I'm crushed by the thought that were she still alive, Gram would probably be disappointed in me right now.

EIGHT

GO

I pick up my phone and smile. FRISBEE GOLF: SPORT OR NOT?

NOT, I send back to Chris, and shake my head. Since I gave him my number he's texted me about a hundred times, but not one phone call. I'm not sure if he's purposely drawing it out or if he'd rather text. But I'd be lying if I said I didn't like the instant satisfaction of writing back and forth all day.

CHEERLEADING: SPORT OR NOT?

TRICK QUESTION, he writes. ARE YOU A CHEER-LEADER?

I lean against the kitchen counter as my dad and Debbie sift through papers, paying bills. Debbie—which is actually what all of her friends call her—is pretty cool about everything, even though I get the sense that she wants to spend more time with me but is afraid to ask. I like her enough . . .

but it still feels sort of traitorous to my mom to just dive into a relationship with my father's new wife. I'm taking it slow.

NOT A CHEERLEADER, I reply to Chris. BUT I HAVE A PRETTY GOOD HIGH KICK. WATCH OUT.

VICIOUS.

I laugh and Dad and Debbie look over, smiling like they're in on the joke somehow. "Is that Simone?" my father asks. My expression falters a little, and I nod.

"Yep. She's sharing some of her latest misadventures." I don't know why I lie to him—there's no reason to. Then again, what if he doesn't think I should date or he has some weird dad ritual for meeting any guy I text? Or maybe I like having a secret. Something I can't be judged for.

"Do you want anything to eat?" Debbie asks. "I can reheat some macaroni." She brushes her auburn hair behind her ear, such a youthful movement that I have to remind myself that she's not *that* much younger than my dad. Still, she's nothing like my mom. At the thought of my mother, I lower my eyes.

"No, thanks. I'm probably going to watch some TV, though."

"Oh, okay. Maybe I'll join you later?"

"Sure." I offer an awkward wave, noticing how my father's forehead creases even though he's pretending to watch the computer screen. I leave the room and head to the couch, falling back without even grabbing the remote.

I'M WRITING YOU A SONG, Chris texts.

I smile so hard my cheeks hurt. REALLY?

UH-HUH. MAYBE I'LL LET YOU HEAR IT SOMETIME. YOU LIKE NEIL DIAMOND, RIGHT?

I laugh. IT'S SWEET CAROLINE, ISN'T IT?

HOW CAN YOU HATE THAT SONG??

BECAUSE WHEN YOUR NAME IS CAROLINE, EVERY-ONE THINKS YOU WANT TO BE SERENADED WITH IT. ALL THE TIME.

I've been hearing that song since I was a kid, from both my family and friends. Except Simone. She hates it nearly as much as I do.

SOUNDS TO ME LIKE IT'S MORE A PROBLEM WITH THEIR LACK OF CREATIVITY, Chris texts.

POSSIBLY. OTHER THAN THIS AMAZING SONG YOU'RE WRITING, ANY OTHER BIG FRIDAY NIGHT PLANS? The minute I hit send, I regret it. Will he think I'm asking him out?

ARE YOU ASKING ME OUT, CAROLINE?

I put my hand over my mouth to stifle my giggle and then dart a look toward the kitchen, wondering if my dad and Debbie can hear my embarrassment all the way in there.

NO. JUST THOUGHT A PARTY STUD LIKE YOURSELF WOULD BE OUT AND NOT TEXTING A STRANGER.

I CAN BE OUT AND STILL TEXT.

My heart dips just a little as I think about Chris demonstrating his superhuman strength for another girl. But then

I think about that party, and how I left my grandmother to go there . . . and I don't really feel like texting anymore. I don't feel like anything.

I'M NOT ACTUALLY OUT, he writes back after I don't immediately reply. STALKING YOUR FACEBOOK PAGE INSTEAD. SHOULD I KEEP THAT DETAIL TO MYSELF?

But I'm no longer in the mood to joke around. I look toward Gram's picture hanging on the wall in the dining room. It's a photo of her and my grandfather, his hand on her shoulder as they both mug for the camera. They were so happy together. I glance down at my phone and scroll the messages, wanting to talk to someone to take my mind off Gram. Realizing how much I need Simone. And remembering that even she doesn't want to talk to me right now.

I HAVE TO GO, I type to Chris. NIGHT.

GOOD NIGHT. NEXT TIME I'LL CALL YOU.

I lie on the couch, tucking the throw pillow under my head as I reach for the remote on the coffee table. My phone buzzes, startling me. But it's not Chris. My mother is calling. I click ignore and then leave my phone at my side—pretending that I don't exist.

NINE

STAY

After our impromptu date at the fairgrounds on Wednesday, Joel turns completely cold, avoiding me in class and in the halls and just flat-out everywhere. It's so unnerving that I become hyperaware of where he is at all times, watching for waves or glances or any indication at all that he did, in fact, have his tongue in my mouth two days ago. The funny thing is that focusing on Joel—even though he's being a complete jerk—is somehow better than focusing on the void in my heart.

The void Gram left behind.

"Bad news," Simone says when she shimmies up next to me at my locker after school on Friday. I look at her, bracing for a blow. Simone was supportive when I told her about my behind-the-scenes romance with Joel, and she said she'd run recon. So . . . bad news isn't exactly what I want to hear.

"Oh, no," I say, leaning in close.

She nods. "Yep. So Joel and Lauren are hanging out this weekend." She does an exaggerated frown like one you'd draw in kindergarten. My heart sinks.

"Well, maybe he's going to break up with her," I say, feigning optimism and hating myself for not just forgetting him altogether. Why do I like someone who had a zillion chances but never took one? Who may or may not like me now because I had a death in the family and he feels some sense of kismet because of it?

"Maybe," Simone says, then, "Yeah, that's gotta be it. I'm sure that's what he's doing. So, hey, what are *we* doing tonight? We could drive to Clinton and make your brother get us into a college party. We haven't done that in ages."

I do want to go visit Teddy sometime, but not this weekend.

"I promised Natalie we'd get pedicures," I say. "So I have to go meet her. But I'll come over later?"

Simone looks at me like I've grown horns. "You're not seriously ditching me for your evil sister."

"I'm not ditching you," I say, starting down the hallway. Simone falls into step. "And maybe lay off Nat, okay? We're both going through the sadness of losing Gram; we get each other better right now. I mean, I know we always used to joke about her, but it's sort of not funny anymore."

"Got it," Simone says, eyes serious. "I . . . I'm sorry. I should've put all that together myself."

"It's okay," I say, relieved.

"No, really. That was beyond lame of me," she says. "Consider Natalie *my* bestie, too."

"Well, you don't have to go that far," I say, "but thanks. And I'll be at your house by seven—I don't want to miss greasy pizza and gossip."

"Don't think for one second that you're forcing me to listen to mopey music all night long."

"It's not mopey; it's soulful," I say, laughing. She eyeballs me.

"Look at you in your cute little Cons with your shoegazer music—you're so emo," she says, bumping me.

"And you're the pop diva," I say, bumping back. "Not everyone is all 'Brittney Banshee is the best thing to ever happen to music!'" I mock.

"Whatever; you love her too."

"I like her. You love her. Like, want-to-dye-your-hair-blue-and-dance-in-rainbows-with-her love."

"Well, you are *way* obsessed with Electric Freakshow. Like, want-to-have-their-punk-rock-babies-with-fauxhawks-and-vintage-T-shirts obsessed."

We both crack up. Simone takes my arm and starts swinging it as we walk. "We're so awesome," she says, starting a round of our long-running extreme self-confidence game.

"We're the prettiest girls at school, and our breath never

smells." I lift my chin and straighten my naturally deflective posture.

"We have the nicest, shiniest hair. We have princess hair!" she says, beaming and stroking her hair like Sleeping Beauty might.

"We are the smartest girls on the planet! Anything we don't know is worthless because we are the taste makers of . . . everything!"

A girl walking in front of us turns around. "Wow," she says, looking us up and down. "You really like yourselves." She flips back around and Simone and I laugh all the way to the student parking lot.

An hour later, I've got my feet in a tub and the massage chair on high. Natalie's squirming in a chair next to me as a woman rubs a pumice stone over her heel: She's super ticklish.

"I hate this part," she says when she realizes I'm looking at her.

"Think of something else," I say. "Read your magazine."

"I can't focus! Distract me!" she pleads.

"Uh . . . okay," I say, trying to think of something to say that isn't about our family; I don't want to talk about Gram. The only other person on my mind is a guy. "You remember Joel Ryder, right?"

"Lauren's boyfriend?" she asks with a curled lip, then squirms in her seat. The woman tells her to hold still.

"You don't like him?" I ask, surprised.

"Not him," she says. "Lauren is devil spawn. She majorly screwed over a good friend of mine last year, and I heard that she's still up to her old ways this year."

"Good," I say, relieved, "because I made out with her boyfriend. Twice."

The cosmetologists stifle giggles. Natalie's eyes widen and her mouth drops open, but I see a hint of amusement like she thinks it's good gossip and not the horrifying kind. Plus she's finally sitting still. She turns her shoulders toward me and leans in a little. "Tell me everything."

For twenty minutes I tell Natalie the story of Joel, from the day we met to my longtime obsession to his out-of-the-blue kiss in the auditorium to the fairgrounds to his giving me the brush-off at school. Nat is completely engrossed in the story—and I can tell by her face that she's absorbing without judgment. Maybe we really have moved past our issues.

When I'm finished, she sighs.

"Okay, so first of all, let's just get one thing straight: That guy's a complete bag," she says, shaking her head. "You're a total catch! I mean, you got Dad's tall, skinny genes—jerk!—and your hair is straight and shiny—I've always coveted it. Plus you're smart and funny—you're the whole package. He's a loser if he's not into you."

"Thanks, Nat," I say, embarrassed. I can't remember the

last time she's given me a compliment, let alone a whole string of them like that. *She likes my hair?*

"Now, I'm not into this whole cheating thing—it's beneath you," she says, managing to sound more friend than parent. "But I've heard gossip about Lauren's exploits at school; the girl's not exactly a one-man woman if you know what I mean. So, don't feel too guilty about her." My shoulders relax a bit before Nat adds, "But seriously, Coco, cheating—whether you're the cheater or the cheatee—only makes you feel bad about yourself." Her eyes hold mine so intently that I think she might have experience in this area. I want to ask whether she's been cheated on, but she keeps going.

"What you need to do is get Joel to tell you how he really feels and then move on from there," she says. "If he was just looking for a hookup, then fine, you can get over that. There's a cute guy in my Spanish class I'll set you up with. But if Joel really likes you—and if he's going to break up with Lauren—then great."

"Thanks. I really . . . it's nice to talk to someone about this stuff." I pause, considering, and then I just go for the sentiment. "It's nice to talk to *you*."

"I wish it didn't take Gram dying to force us into hanging out again," she says with a sad smile. "But I'm glad we got here one way or another."

"Me too," I say.

The massage feature on my chair stops abruptly, and I reach over to restart it. I look back at Natalie, thinking that I might tell her I love her, but she's already reading about the latest celebrity breakup while the pedicurist paints her toenails bright red. So, I leave it alone for now.

"Can I tell you something, and you promise not to judge me?" I ask later at Simone's house, just before taking the biggest bite of pizza known to man.

"Shoot," Simone says, distracted by a magazine she's flipping through.

"I'm embarrassed about the whole Joel thing," I say, lowering my eyes. "Both that I fell for his tortured soul routine and the fact that I'm super sad that he didn't leave his plastic girlfriend for me. I'm a horrible person, right?"

"Not nearly as horrible as I'd be." She grins. When I don't laugh, she throws her arm over my shoulders in a side hug. "Linus, you're easily the nicest person I know. Joel fed you some lines—lame ones, but whatever—and you believed him. I'm pretty sure that makes him the jerkoff in this scenario."

"I guess," I say. Simone pulls away and grabs her own slice of pizza. "Before Gram died," I start again, "she told me to be careful of who I love, to not let them take too much."

"Gram was a smart lady," Simone says through a mouth full of food.

I smile. "Yeah. She was. She also told me to not let a bad choice ruin my life. Does Joel count as one of those?"

"Definitely."

I nod, thinking it over. I'm not in love with Joel, even though I've dreamed of him for years. But if it can still hurt this much, I can't imagine how much *real* love must suck.

"You know," Simone adds, "I'm reading an interview in *Rolling Stone* with the lead singer of Electric Freakshow, and he said he wrote their last song about the whole concept of choices and where they lead." She smiles. "Maybe Gram read that same article."

"Yeah," I say. "I'm sure River Devlin was a huge source of inspiration for her."

"Anything's possible." When she leaves to grab us Cokes, I feel unsettled. Because I can still hear the sorrow in Gram's voice when she said, "Never let them take what's *you.*"

I resolve at that second to end this drama with Joel, to stop sneaking around, to stop waiting for him. I won't let him take what's me. So later that night, after the room falls quiet with only Simone's soft snoring in the air, I sit up, throw off the covers, and use my phone to guide me out into the hallway. Then, I type, without thinking, what I need to say to him.

IT'S CRAP THAT YOU IGNORED ME FOR TWO DAYS. WE NEED TO TALK—OR ACTUALLY, YOU DO. WHAT DO YOU WANT?

I hit send before my rational side realizes what's happening. After it's gone, I go back and reread the text—that's when the worrying starts. I stare at my phone for a full two minutes, willing it to chime.

He's with Lauren—of course he's not answering my texts.

Spending time with Natalie and then Simone must have pumped me up enough to harden my heart—even a little—because although I'm aware of the taste of rejection in the back of my mouth, I'm happy that I sent the message. At least he knows what's on my mind. At least he knows I'm not some pathetic wimp. Maybe I dodged a bullet here.

I creep back into Simone's room and climb under the air bed covers. And this time, I fall asleep.

When I wake to Simone's mom's heels clicking on the hardwood floors at seven the next morning, I stretch and yawn and smile at the ceiling—it was a peaceful rest. But my blood pressure rises when I tap on my phone: At two in the morning, Joel wrote back. It's just one word, but it sends shivers down my spine—and in the light of the new day, my girl power faded from sleep, I'm not sure whether they're the bad or the good kind.

YOU.

NINE

GO

Saturday evening, I'm loading the dishwasher when my phone rings from the counter. My stress level climbs as I lean over and check the caller ID, worried it's my mother, who I haven't spoken to, or wondering if it could be Chris, who has yet to actually call me.

When I see it's Simone, I swallow hard. I never called her back after our last conversation. My hand is actually shaking when I bring the phone to my ear.

"Hey, Mony," I say, trying to sound like everything's fine. She's quick to squash that lie.

"Oh, hey," she responds with fake peppiness. "Guessing you're not coming out tonight—seeing as you're not here. But that's okay. I'm getting used to you bailing."

"The party." I close my eyes, remembering that I agreed

weeks ago to show up at Alan Fritz's annual October bash. "I'm sorry," I say. "I forgot; I would've—"

"Would you have, Caroline?" The hurt is thick in her voice, and although I know it's my fault, I'm not sure what to say. "You said you were moving to your dad's to deal, but all I know is that you seem to have cut me out of your life. I'm drowning here without you. I—" She chokes up, and I lower my head, feeling horrible for how I've been treating her.

"I'm sorry," I whisper. "I don't want to fight."

"Don't you see that that's the problem?" she asks, her voice picking up a higher pitch. "You never fight for anything. Stand up for your goddamn self and fix things."

Her words tick me off, maybe because I know they're partly true. "You sound like Natalie."

"Yeah? Well, at least your sister isn't leaving her friends to live in some guilt-free fantasy world."

"It's far from guilt free," I snap back. My father pokes his head in the room, surveying my stance at the dishwasher before retreating back into the living room.

"Staying there isn't going to make it better," Simone says. "I wish you could just see that."

I'm silent for a long time, and Simone waits. I almost expect her to hang up on me, but then I remind myself that Simone would never hang up on me. And she'd never cut me out of her life. Not for anything. I let my anger roll away, shove it away, so that I can claim back a little bit of myself.

"Do you still want me to go to that party with you?" I ask. "I'll drive back right now." I realize that I mean it.

"No," she says, her voice softer. "Alan's lame anyway. But maybe you can call more often. Or at least acknowledge that you still care about me."

"Mony, you're my best friend. I'll come home tomorrow, okay? We'll . . . we'll go out for fro-yo or something."

She laughs, and the sound of it makes me smile. "Bribing me with frozen treats?" she asks. "You know the way to my heart. Speaking of heart, I thought you should know that Joel Ryder has not only been asking about you, but that he and Lauren have ended their star-crossed romance. Looks like he's wide open for you."

I wait for a flutter, a tingle, anything to happen. But my heart is calm. "Actually," I say. "I think I might be over him."

Simone's gasp is long and dramatic. "You little minx. You've met a boy, haven't you?"

I lean against the granite counter, grinning as I tell Simone the details of my random encounters with Chris. She's riveted, enough so that she forgives me for being a coward. If only I could forgive myself.

Simone makes me promise that tomorrow will be just us— no other friends or hot guys—and that I have to re-create my entire life through charades so she doesn't feel left out. When I agree, we hang up.

I stand at the sink for a while. The dishes done, the house quiet, I let myself think of Gram. It was just a few weeks ago when I told her I was sick of doing the dishes and that we should start using paper plates. She smiled from her comfy chair, still sorting through the ads in the Sunday paper. She told me that dishwashing would make me a better person. I told her it worked both ways.

Then my seventy-five-year-old grandmother came over and took the sponge from my hand. She brushed back my hair and told me to finish my homework.

I burst into tears, wishing for even one moment back. One irrelevant moment. My shoulders shake with my cries, but then I hear the clank of the washing machine lid in the other room.

I wipe quickly at my face and turn the knob of the dishwasher, filling the room with a familiar *whoosh*. I wipe down the counter and then wander out of the kitchen in search of life. In search of distraction. I find Dad and Debbie in the laundry room.

"For the millionth time, the soap goes in *here*," Debbie is saying, her voice teasing, not exasperated like Mom's always used to be when schooling Dad on housework. Debbie isn't nearly as stereotypically evil as a stepmother should be. And it's clear that she really does love my father. Even if he seems to be clueless half the time.

"Hi," I say from the doorway. They both look up and smile. "Dishes are done."

"You didn't smash any?" my father asks, acknowledging the fight he witnessed.

"No. Simone and I just had to work through some things. We're cool now. I'm going to visit her tomorrow."

"Thank you so much for helping out around the house, Caroline," Debbie says warmly. "You really didn't have to do that."

"Yes, thank you, Coco," Dad says, and the sound of my childhood nickname from him feels nice. "You saved me from having to do it ... wrong." He smirks at Debbie; she swats him.

"You load with no order," she says.

"There's a method to my madness," he counters. "You just can't see it."

"No one could see it," she says, laughing. Then she remembers I'm standing there. "We're going to watch a movie; would you like to join us?"

Although at one time that thought might have made me cringe, now it actually seems comforting—almost like a hug. "I'd like that," I say, a little timidly. "Let me just go upstairs and change. I'll be back in a few." I turn to leave them with their linens.

"Oh, and Caroline?" Dad says, more serious this time. I turn to face him. "Your mom called again today. She'd really like to talk to you. Maybe you want to give her a ring before the movie?"

"I'll call her tomorrow," I say, then turn and walk away.

I've only talked to my mother once in the past three days; I might never speak to my sister again. Teddy has been keeping me up to date on the goings-on with Gram's estate—which is leading up to a battle between my mom and aunt since Gram's will wasn't that clear. The thought turns my stomach, my grandmother's possessions being sorted through and fought over, proving she's never coming back.

An hour later I'm settled in, watching the movie with Dad and Debbie—on a Saturday night—when my phone rings. I grin from ear to ear when I see Chris's number. He's finally calling.

"Hello?" I ask.

"Sweet Caroline. Bah da da. Good times never seem so good—"

I hang up and cover my mouth as I laugh. I told him not to sing that damn song. He must have continued his chorus for a while because my phone doesn't ring again for a few minutes. My father glances over at me, his finger on the pause button, but I tell him to go on without me. Then I take my phone to my room.

"I thought we had a deal," I say the minute I answer.

"I said I would try. I have amazing willpower, but tonight, I just couldn't resist."

"You're a terrible singer," I say. I stop in front of my dresser mirror, sliding my hair behind my ear; there's already a blush high on my cheeks.

"Since karaoke's out," Chris says, "where would you like to go on our date?"

"I don't remember agreeing to a date."

"You don't remember asking me out?" He pretends to be surprised. "You seemed pretty insistent, and I interpreted that to mean that you're completely and hopelessly in love with me. Did I read too much into it?"

"Wow."

"In fact, I thought we both decided this was fate. And believe me, Caroline. You don't want to tempt fate." He sighs. "I think we have no choice but to see this thing through. It will be difficult, but I think we'll persevere in the face of—"

"Oh my God. If I say yes, will you shut up?"

"Yep."

I close my eyes, biting back my smile. "Since I'm new in town, maybe you should pick where we go. But nothing fancy."

"Would it worry you if I said I already had an idea?"

"Uh, yeah."

"I'll pick you up in a half hour."

. . .

I find the most date-worthy outfit I have—a denim skirt with tights and black boots paired with a soft black sweater. It's actually dressier than I thought, especially when I twist my hair up into a knot. I take the time to apply makeup, something I haven't done since my grandmother—

I stop the thought, shaking my hands at my side to wave away the pain. When it clears, when I can breathe again, I avoid my reflection and head downstairs, determined to have a good night.

The moment is odd, me standing in the entry of the living room as my father and his new wife snuggle next to each other on the couch. I swallow down the lump in my throat, remembering that my parents actually used to love each other—but now they love other people. It's tragic and sad and I look away as I call to him.

"Dad, do you mind if I go out with a friend?"

I hear the blanket rustle and when I look back, he's standing there. "Which friend?" The *dad* in his voice throws me.

"He's . . . he's a friend from back home. He goes to school here and he wanted to hang out for a couple hours. If I can't or whatever, it's fine. I just need to—"

"You're seventeen years old, Caroline," he says, bewildered. "You're allowed to have friends." Debbie gets up to stand behind him, wrapping her arms playfully over his shoulders as she grins at me.

"Is this a date?" she asks.

I want to flat-out lie—save myself the embarrassment—but I don't this time. I roll my eyes. "Sort of. But it's nothing serious. I barely know him." My dad's eyebrows quirk up. "I mean I know him," I correct quickly. "But we're not like—" I stop, aware that I'm losing this word battle. "It's our first date."

"You like him," Debbie teases. "Is he coming now? Can I peek out the window when he pulls up?"

"Please don't," I mumble, but she and my father are already at the curtain, pulling it aside as they whisper to each other. It gets me how cutesy they are, as if the idea of having a kid around makes them giddy. Then I remember that my brother told me they've been trying to have a baby. Maybe that's why they're directing all this parental involvement on me—practice.

"What kind of car does he drive?" my father asks.

I shrug. "No idea. But I hope the windows are tinted dark."

"I bet he drives a Toyota," Debbie says, brushing her hair away from her face. "A silver one."

"Why would you think that?" I ask.

"Because he's parked out front." She widens her eyes at me. "Very cute, Caroline."

I'm washed in the kind of humiliation that I thought only

my grandmother could bring out in me. The sadness hits again with sudden ferocity; I wish Gram were here to tease me instead. The joy of the moment fades away, and I tell Dad and Debbie that I'll be home by eleven before grabbing my jacket.

I walk out, rethinking this entire adventure, when Chris gets out of the car, watching me over the hood. "I forgot the corsage," he says smiling. "But we can still take photos if you like."

"Not that kind of date, Christopher," I say, glancing back to catch my stepmother in the window. She waves politely and then lets the curtain fall shut.

Chris's goofy grin transforms into something more serious. I pause at the door. "What?" I ask.

"You're gorgeous," he murmurs.

I stare at him, my stomach fluttering as I fight back the urge to giggle. "You say it like you're surprised."

"Oh, I'm not," he says. "I know you're beautiful. I'm just not sure why you'd agree to go out with me."

"I'm the one who asked, remember?" I smile. "And what's with this false modesty? You seem to be fully aware of your charisma."

Chris comes around the car to open my door, making my breath catch with his sudden proximity, the heat that radiates from his body to mine. Under his jacket he's wearing a button-down plaid shirt, his hair is combed smooth, and he smells *amazing.* It strikes me that I'm on a grown-up date, not the sort of party hookup that Simone finds herself involved in. My nerves start to twist as I duck inside Chris's car, then lift my gaze to his. I vow to leave my guilt behind—if only for tonight.

"So where are we going?" I ask as Chris drives us through the darkened streets. "It's not some sketchy underground karaoke club, is it?"

"Not on a first date," he says like I'm crazy. "I save that sort of thing for anniversaries." Chris turns into the parking lot of a small coffee shop and cuts the engine. "I thought we'd go to the park."

"To the park? Uh, you know it's cold enough to snow, right?"

"We'll have hot chocolate, *obviously.*" He motions to the building in front of us. "Besides, it's beautiful at night. I think you'll like it." He says it quietly, as if he's really thought about it. I want to reach over and take his hand—something I wouldn't normally do. This all seems different, though, easier. Or maybe I'm just desperate for a distraction.

Chris and I go inside and get a couple of large cocoas, along with a slice of pumpkin pie, extra whipped cream. Once it's packaged up, we drive to Cedar Hills Park a few blocks away. He takes the drink carrier and pie, and I steal glances at him as we walk across the grounds; he has an amused smile on his lips the entire time.

"What's with the corny grin?" I ask as he leads us down the paved walkway.

"Corny?" he says. "This is my victory grin." Chris stops at a park bench overlooking the huge pond with a fountain in the middle. Lights turn the mist from blue to red to green, and I think that he's right. It is beautiful.

"Is this where you take all of your dates?" I ask playfully when I sit down next to him. He looks over, surprised.

"No." He hands me a hot chocolate, and the cup is warm, taking the chill away even as I breathe out puffs of white air. "Just you."

There's a flutter in my stomach, and I look down into my lap to hide the blush on my cheeks. "Are you always this charming?"

"Absolutely."

"I'm sure you're very popular on campus," I say, taking a sip from my hot drink. "And at parties from what you tell me." He laughs.

"Are you asking if I've had a lot of girlfriends?"

"Uh, no."

Chris leans back against the green-painted bench. "Yes you were. And the answer is yes, I've had a lot, but nothing serious."

"Maybe you *should* have taken them here, then," I mutter, earning another laugh. To be honest, I'm glad he doesn't have an ex to be hung up on.

"You're such a smart-ass." Only he says it like it's his

favorite thing in the world. Chris looks away and I watch as the lights dance across his face. He's so comfortable— even confident. I wish he'd put his arm around me, snuggle into me, anything. And then I think that I've never been so attracted to anyone in my life. He turns to meet my stare.

"See, it's not so cold," he murmurs.

"Not now." We both grin before he unwraps the pie and hands me a fork. I immediately dip it into the whipped cream and then lick the edge. I hope it looks flirtatious, but Chris only side-eyes me before knocking his knee against mine.

"Let's talk about you," he says. "What's a secret wish that you've never told anybody?"

"Shouldn't we build up to secrets?"

He shakes his head. "No. That's where we start. Now spill one or I'm taking the pie." He grabs the container and holds it away from us.

"Bully," I say. I consider clutching my fork like a butcher knife, pretending to stab him, but I'm not sure if we've reached the joking-murder point in our relationship. I decide instead to cross my arms over my chest—up for a willpower challenge. When he sees I'm not going to budge, he reluctantly lowers the plate to set it back on his leg.

"You win," he concedes. "But you still have to tell me your wish."

"How will you even know if it's really a secret?" I ask.

"I'll just have to trust you."

I like his answer. There isn't anyone else in my life who would say that to me right now. I exhale, thinking of any wish worth mentioning. "Hm . . . I guess I wish I was fluent in French, like my sister Natalie," I say.

"Aw, what?" Chris calls out. "That's like . . . such an over-achiever thing to say. No fair. You have to be embarrassed to make it count."

I push him. "Whatever. What's yours?"

He catches my hand and runs his gaze over me, his smile fading when he meets my eyes. "I wish I had the guts to kiss you right now."

It knocks me out: The way he says it sends my body into an absolute free fall. "Then why don't you?" I ask, surprised at my own boldness.

He takes his hand reluctantly from mine. "I'm shy."

I laugh loudly. "Christopher, you are not shy. Not even a little."

"Not normally," he says. "Just with you. It's completely unsettling." He smiles. "But thrilling as hell." He looks embarrassed, and I decide he's right—it does count more.

I poke at the pie with my fork to do something other than stare and smile at him. At this moment everything is right—the stars have aligned or some other romantic crap. I'm totally lost in him.

Chris moves closer, his thigh against mine. "Although I appreciate the encouragement," he says, "you don't exactly strike me as the kissing-random-guys-on-park-benches type."

"You don't really know me all that well. . . ."

"Not yet," he says seriously, before turning back to the pond. "But I will. Until then I want to play hard to get a little longer."

"Tease." I shove him sideways. Chris doesn't bring up kissing me again, but just the mention was enough to make my body downright warm, even in the frigid weather. We stay a while longer, talking and not talking, comfortable either way.

And as we get up to leave, he takes my hand.

TEN

STAY

Monday morning before school, Mom, Natalie, and I scramble to finish boxing up Gram's stuff and separating it before the Salvation Army truck comes. We've been here since five in the morning; I haven't gotten up that early since . . . forever. Yawning, I reach from the ladder I'm standing on to grab another bin from the high shelf in Gram's closet.

"I can't find her necklace," Natalie says from over near the dresser. "Have you seen it? I hope we didn't accidentally pack it."

"Which?" I ask, my arms elbow deep in tiny paper.

"The one she always wore—the one with her initials on it?" she says. "It's not in here. You don't think Aunt Claudia took it, do you?"

My stomach sinks. The necklace is in my dresser drawer at home. It was Gram's favorite—the one that I used to twist and twirl while she read me bedtime stories when I was little. It's gold and classic-looking and not my style . . . but it's her. It's mine.

"Why do you want it?" I ask, stalling. Nat looks away from me when she answers.

"She told me to keep it," she says quietly. "The night she died. Because we have the same initials and everything."

I want to cry in that way when you do when something is so unfair, but you know you have to do it anyway. Overtired and distracted by how conflicted I am, I teeter on the ladder. I reach out and grab for the high shelf to steady myself, but it's not bolted into the wall, and it teeters too. I fall from three steps up and land with a loud thud on Gram's carpeted closet floor.

"Oh my God, are you okay?" Natalie says, rushing over. She holds out a hand and pulls me up, her concern shaming me even more. "What happened?"

"Freaking ladder is wobbly," I say, brushing my backside even though I didn't fall into anything dirty. "But I'm fine." I touch my right hip—it's tender. "Ouch, that's going to leave a wicked bruise."

"You have to be careful," Nat says, shaking her head and returning to the dresser. "Jeez, I thought I had the gold medal in klutziness."

"Well, you did fly over the handlebars of your bike and

skid across pavement on your face that time," I say, righting the ladder and climbing back up, holding on to the door frame to ensure I don't fall again.

She laughs and shakes her head at herself. Then we fall into a silent moment; I know it's almost time to leave for school.

"I'll keep my eye out for the necklace," I lie quietly, not ready to give up my piece of Gram just yet.

"Thanks, Coco," Natalie says, a far-off sadness in her eyes. I can see how much she wants the necklace, how much it would mean to her—but I decide to keep it anyway.

Joel passes me a note after first period. He walks away without words, leaving me stupefied. I haven't heard anything since his one-word text on Friday night—YOU—and now he's back and passing me notes like a seventh grader?

For some reason I don't want to read what he wrote in front of Simone, so I linger in the English classroom after everyone else is gone and peek at the note when I'm alone.

Meet me in the auditorium at lunch.

I can't help it; my heart races. I shove the paper in my jeans pocket and walk into the hall, looking in the direction that he went, but he's gone. I head to my locker, figuring that I'll find out what's going on soon enough.

The next few periods aren't exactly prime learning hours for me. With distractions of Joel, I go through the motions, just hoping no one calls on me. Thankfully, we watch a movie in history and it's a work period in art, and Mrs. Marks is out sick and our science sub blabs on without interacting with any of us. When the bell rings, instead of hitting my locker, I text Simone.

MEETING JOEL. TEXT YOU LATER.

She texts back, WWGS?

??

WHAT WOULD GRAM SAY?

I pause, thinking it over. Then I write, SHE'D TELL ME TO BE CAREFUL.

ONCE AGAIN, SHE'S A SMART LADY.

I smile and put away my phone. Simone's right. Gram's right. I need to be strong and, most of all, careful. I make my way to the place that's apparently become mine and Joel's: the auditorium. When I arrive, I don't see him. I walk down the center aisle toward the stage; when I'm visible from the balcony above, I hear his voice.

"Hi, Caroline," he says, startling me. I turn and find him peering over the edge of the balcony. "Come up?" he asks.

"Okay." I walk over to the stairs near the right side of the room and climb slowly so I won't be out of breath when I get there. He's waiting at the top, and the second my foot hits the landing, he grabs my hand and pulls me close.

"I'm happy to see you," he says, which strikes me as odd since we spent first period together this morning. But still, I hug back. He burrows his face into my hair and takes a deep breath.

"You smell good," he says in a low tone that stirs something inside me. I consider kissing him—his kisses are like salted caramel hot chocolate—before remembering the drama from last week. I put my hands on his shoulders and push back a foot.

"Hey, Joel?" I say. "What are we doing here?"

He looks at me for a few seconds, then steps back and takes my hand. "Come here." We walk to seats in the front row, overlooking the section where we sat the first time we came here. When we're settled, he wastes no time. "I broke it off with Lauren this weekend."

Relief floods through me; Natalie was right that cheating makes you feel awful about yourself. I'm so glad that it's over.

"Does that make you happy?" he asks, looking into my eyes.

"I think so," I say honestly. Just because they broke up doesn't mean we're—

"I did it for you," he says. "I like you, Caroline. I can't stop thinking about you . . . your hair, your lips. The way you taste. I want to draw you."

I consider that all of Joel's compliments are surface—they're about the way I look. But, trusting that there has to be more in his heart, I allow myself to feel flattered. To crush hard on him.

"Anytime."

"You mean it?"

"Hey, it looked cool when Kate and Leo did it."

"Huh?" he asks, not getting my *Titanic* reference.

"Never mind," I say, wondering if any two people are ever really perfectly connected with each other. Maybe understanding someone to the point that you can practically hear his or her soul is just stuff of books and super-expensive movies.

"Friday night?" he asks, moving on. "My parents will be out. My stepdad has some charity thing and they're sleeping over. I'm sure they're planning to get hammered—at least they're smart enough not to drive."

"Sure, sounds amazing," I say, wondering if going to Joel's house so he can draw me qualifies as a first date. Or maybe we already had our first date? At the fairgrounds? And does this mean we're dating now? I spin on mechanics and milestones until Joel takes my face in his hands and kisses me. There's so much I want to ask about—his weekend, his family, his *life*—but my words are corked by kisses.

When the warning bell rings and the lunch period is over, we pull apart and move downstairs to the nearby bathrooms to make ourselves presentable. In the mirror, I examine my red chin and lips, my flushed cheeks and mussed hair.

Is this all we are? No, there has to be more.

I find Joel leaning against lockers in the deserted hallway between the auditorium and the Family Sciences wing. I walk up and stop in front of him; he hooks his fingers through my belt loops.

"That was better than the lunch special," he says, a sparkle in his eyes. And then he actually smiles. The sight of his straight white teeth makes my heart rate quicken; I smile so hard my face might crack.

"Yeah," I say. "It was fun."

Joel leans in and kisses me gently on the forehead, then brushes it away with his thumb. "You can go first," he says. "I'll wait here a minute."

"What do you mean?" I ask, looking toward the mouth of the hallway and back into Joel's eyes. He tilts his head to the side just a hair, confused.

"Just being chivalrous," he says with a shrug.

"But . . . I . . . ," I say, piecing it together like a particularly complicated puzzle that my brain just can't quite grasp. Finally it hits me. "You mean you don't want to walk out together?"

"Uh . . . ," he says. "We probably shouldn't, right?" He steps a little closer, gripping even tighter on my jeans. "The body's not even cold on my relationship with Lauren. She's still got a lot of friends here. I don't want her to think I've been messing around on her."

But you have! I want to scream. I bite my tongue.

"I mean I don't think we should tell anyone about us just yet, do you?" he asks in as sweet a voice as I've ever heard from him. "You mean a lot to me, and I don't want people thinking you're just my rebound girl. I want us to be able to be a thing . . . a real thing."

"Just not yet," I say. I mean it sarcastically, but there's no weight to my words. He thinks I'm agreeing.

"Soon," he says, kissing me lightly on the lips and then releasing his hold on my pants. He raises a chin toward the main hallway, where a few students pass by. "You'd better get going. Don't want to be late."

I take a step back, baffled by what's happening and even more by the fact that I'm letting it happen. "Guess I'll see you around."

"Don't forget about Friday," he says. "I can't wait to spend a whole night alone with you."

I wave and fake a smile before turning my back on him. I walk up the dark corridor and into the well-lit main hallway, feeling like I just returned from planet Who The Hell Am I?, wondering when I signed up to be someone's secret plaything and hating myself for loving the smell of Joel's body still lingering on my clothes.

TEN

GO

Clinton High School is smaller than my old school, a one-story brick building with a thick set of woods behind it. As I park, I survey the people walking in—checking out their clothes, seeing how they interact. I figure out that thirty miles doesn't make a big fashion difference, but it does make me a complete outsider. Slowly I climb out of the car, ready to face the isolation of new girl syndrome.

After getting my schedule from the front office, I make my way to homeroom. The class is mostly empty, and the teacher isn't in the room yet. I stand around, and when no one offers a spot next to them, I take a seat near the front and wait. My phone vibrates.

DON'T MAKE ANY NEW BEST FRIENDS, Simone writes, and I smile. When we met up yesterday for fro-yo, things were a bit awkward at first. We didn't talk about the party, or Gram, or even the fight we had on the phone. Instead she told me that Joel Ryder continues to ask about me like I've somehow transformed into his version of "the one who got away."

So I told her about my date with Chris. How I like it at my dad's house, but how being there is a little like visiting a distant planet with aliens shaped as parents. And then the normalness of our friendship started to soak in.

"You're in my seat," a girl says as she hovers over the desk. I apologize and stand, not sure where to go. I think about asking the girl, but her severe ponytail and heavily lined eyes sort of scare me, so I go stand in the back of the room near the bookshelf. Every person who walks in takes a good long look at me like I'm this month's class pet. I fidget with the zipper of my backpack to keep from gawking like an idiot.

My teacher, Mr. Powell, finally comes in just as the bell rings. His plaid sports coat is wrinkled at the bottom, and I guess that he's one of those eccentric-type teachers who will make us do trust exercises and share our feelings. As if reading my mind, he comes to a dramatic halt in front of the room.

"A new student?" he asks, holding out his hand. "How lucky are we?"

There are a couple of snickers around the room, and I shrink back as if I can fade into the wall of literary posters. My new friend Miss Severity turns back to look at me, one perfectly arched eyebrow raised. From her sour expression, she doesn't like what she sees.

"Why don't you take the seat right here," Mr. Powell says, pointing to the desk nearest to him. I close my eyes for a moment, trying to gather some bravery before slowly making my way down the aisle. Just when I think my humiliation is about to end, my foot catches the edge of a backpack and I stumble, smacking into the desk of a dude in a red varsity jacket. I fall on top of him, my leg caught on his bag, as I land with my face close enough to kiss him. He smiles a big jock smile as if I did it on purpose and then takes me by the hips to guide me up.

"It's nice to meet you too," he says, earning laughter and catcalls from around the room.

Gross. "Sorry," I mutter, backing out of his arms. When I turn, I see Miss Severity's jaw harden, her eyes narrowed to slits. I'm going to go ahead and guess that I just groped her boyfriend. Not good.

With the weight of her glare intimidating me, I sink down in the front seat, wondering if the day can get any worse. And then, when a paper ball pegs the back of my head, I decide that it most certainly can.

I sit alone in the lunchroom and scroll through my phone for a number. No one looked even remotely interested in sharing a meal with me when I walked in, so I took my brown bag and found the only solo table at the very rear of the room. Fitting, since I feel like an ass already.

"Does this mean you've been thinking about me all day?" Chris says as a way of answering the phone. Instantly I'm better.

"Maybe. Or maybe I already tried Simone and she's in class. And maybe I have no one else to talk to because I'm the weird new girl."

"You're weird in the best ways." He pauses. "That bad, huh?"

"Awful. Today sucks."

"I'm sorry. Would it make you feel better if I told you that I have a three-hour lecture in twenty minutes but am more than willing to skip it? For you."

"Ha! No way," I tell him. "If I have to suffer through an education, so do you."

"Mean."

I smile, finally relaxing now that Chris reminded me that I'm not the complete loser I felt like this morning. "Thanks," I say softly. "Don't read too much into this, but you're a really great life distraction."

"You're so in love with me."

I smile. "Shut up."

The phone shifts and I picture him stretching out on his

bed, grinning like a total doofus, sort of like I am now.

"Hey, you know what would be awesome?" he says, his voice a little lower. "If you'd come over tonight. I'm fully stocked with ramen noodles and Mountain Dew."

"Ew. So I'll bring pizza?"

"Sounds good. Call you when I get out of class."

When we hang up, I look around the cafeteria one more time. I find Miss Severity sitting with her letterman, saying something dramatic, judging by her hand gestures. Just then she notices me, her eyes locking me in place as she leans her head to whisper to one of her equally severe friends. They laugh, watching me the entire time.

I lower my eyes, pretending that my peanut butter sandwich is the most interesting food on the planet. And for the first time I realize that running away hasn't gotten rid of my problems. It's only given me new ones.

Chris's room is neater than I imagined: a single with an organized desk, a television, and, of course, a bed. His door is partly open as he sits back against his pillows with an acoustic guitar in his lap. What he's strumming sounds suspiciously like "Sweet Caroline," but he changes the melody the minute he notices me.

"Hey," he says, smiling broadly. "And you really did bring pizza." I hold up the box and move inside, feeling a prickle of nervousness as I close the door behind me. He looks adorable in his Clinton T-shirt and jeans, so carefree and easy.

"I brought sustenance," I say, holding out the food to him. "But you only get a slice on one condition."

He grins. "Do I have to get undressed?"

"Not exactly where I was going there, Chris. The condition is that you can't ask me about school, varsity jackets, or mean girls who decide on sight that they despise me."

Chris widens his eyes like he can understand just how bad the day has been, and then he reaches for the pizza box to set it aside on his desk. When he straightens, sitting on the edge of his bed, he takes my hands and tugs me toward him.

What starts as a move of seduction quickly changes when he balls my right hand into a fist. "I should teach you how to fight," he says. He pantomimes my fist hitting his cheek in slow motion, along with sound effects and a drawn-out "Nooo . . ." I laugh, thinking he's possibly the silliest person I know, and yet I find it completely endearing.

"Like you know how to fight," I say when he finally finishes knocking himself out.

"I've been in fights," he responds. "Actually, I've been in quite a few." Chris pushes my hip until I sit down next to him, and then he grabs his guitar and starts strumming again. "Believe it or not," he says between chords, "I used to be a troublemaker."

"Lies."

He glances sideways. "I swear it's true. This face you're so fond of has been punched a multitude of times."

"And you're going to teach me the fine art of physical altercations? Doesn't sound like you've gotten the hang of it yet." I'm still not totally buying his sordid *Outsiders* past.

"I may not start the fights." Chris sets the guitar behind him on the bed. "But I always win. I play dirty, Caroline."

I'm pretty sure his admission wasn't meant to make me hot, but I find myself completely ready to wrestle him to the ground. The sinful gleam in his baby blue eyes does little to suppress my urge.

"Wanna fight?" he asks with a grin.

"Oh, yeah."

What I think will turn into a roll-around-on-the-floor-until-we-start-kissing match ends up more like an actual self-defense class. Chris even lets me take a swing at him, which I'll admit is kind of exhilarating, but he dodges it easily before tackling me back onto the bed.

"Let's try that again," he says, climbing up from the mattress. "I can do this all night."

Though it's not *exactly* the way I'd choose to relieve tension, our play fighting is fun, and the day vastly improves. At least until I get home. There's a note next to the phone in my stepmother's cursive.

Caroline,

Natalie called here looking for you. She said to call her and that it's important.

Seeing my sister's name sends me into a panic attack. My mind spins with questions: Is everyone okay? What does she want? What will she say to me this time?

My stomach is sick as I pick up the house phone and dial her number. She answers on the first ring, and I'm rooted in place when her voice hits me. "You selfish brat," she says immediately. "Mom calls your phone three times a day and you have yet to answer her. She's frantic. What the hell is wrong with you?"

Then I remember why I'm here: I ruined my family, starting all the way back to when I was twelve years old. And my sister has never let me forget it. My eyes tear up, and I softly drop the phone on its charger, hanging up on her. I back away slowly, as if it's a snake, and my new life begins to crumble.

I'm such a traitor—playing happy while Gram is dead. I nearly fall apart thinking that it's possible that she would hate me now, too. I dash upstairs to my bed and then curl up in my fake room. My fake life. I'm drowning in guilt and despair, and when I close my eyes, all I can hear is my sister's whisper.

Runner.

ELEVEN
STAY

Climbing the steps to Joel's front porch, I'm approaching basket case status. At only seven, it's already midnight black—thanks, winter—which adds to my jumpiness. But mostly, it's my thoughts that are poking and provoking me. Joel wants to draw me. He likes to make out. And his mom will be gone all night long.

I twist the bracelet on my wrist, hearing Gram tell me to take a belly breath to calm down. I put my right hand on my stomach and inhale, then quickly rip my hand away when the front door opens. Joel's half smiling in a black T-shirt and jeans, sock footed and scruffy. He pretty much looks exactly how I picture him in daydreams.

"Ready to be immortalized?" he asks.

"As long as you're not planning to bite my neck."

He looks at me funny as he shifts in the doorway. Then, "I can't promise anything."

. . .

As it turns out, posing for a sketch is incredibly boring.

"Stop moving," Joel says seriously without looking at my face—he's focused on my hands. I'm sitting on the floor, arms wrapped around my knees, regretting picking this particular position. My butt hurts and my face itches and I'm getting thirsty.

"How about that break?" I ask, trying to shift without him noticing. I imagine myself scratching my cheek—it makes the itch fade a little.

"In a minute," he says, "promise. I just need to get your fingers right." That's what he said a half hour ago about my wrists.

When a break finally comes at nine o'clock, I stand up, creaky, and follow Joel to the kitchen. He offers me a beer, but I reach around him into the fridge and grab a soda instead. Then I wander, looking at the hanging décor and knickknacks. The design is rustic country, and the whole house smells like Joel.

"Want to go up to my room?" he asks, and I can tell from his face that he's really asking if I want to go roll around in his bed with him. I'm sure that he and Lauren had buckets of sex—maybe that's why his version of getting acquainted tends to skew dirty. Truthfully, the fact that his parents are gone all night terrifies me: There's no school bell to ring and tell us to stop.

That would be my job.

"How about we just watch some TV," I say. "I can't stay that much longer—I have to be home at ten."

"You have to be home at ten on a Friday night?" he asks, walking over to the couch and dropping onto it, then sighing and running his hand through his short hair.

"Not usually," I say. "But with everything that's going on with my family . . ." I feel guilty for lying—Mom wouldn't care if I stayed out until midnight—and for using Gram as an excuse to leave.

I join Joel on the couch. He flips on the TV and changes channels a few dozen times; finally he stops on a movie I don't recognize. He grabs my hand and kisses my palm gently.

"You think this night was lame, don't you?"

"No," I say automatically, then, "well, maybe a little."

"Sorry," he says, kissing the inside of my wrist and making my whole arm tingle. "I can't talk and draw at the same time." He kisses the crook opposite my elbow and lingers there a minute. I feel his breath on the blond hairs on my arm: It gives me goose bumps.

"Tell me something I don't know about you," I say, willing myself to have a conversation with this guy instead of pulling him on top of me like I want to right now.

"Like what?" Another kiss on the crook, a fresh set of goose bumps over the ones that hadn't quite gone away.

"Anything," I say, but it comes out as a whisper. I clear my throat. "Anything. I mean, I've known you forever—since your Spider-Man-themed birthday party with the climbing web and comic book favors—but I don't feel like I *know* you."

"I'm no good at this stuff," he says, using two fingers to push up the sleeve of my T-shirt so he can kiss my shoulder. I deserve a medal for remaining still after that one. "Ask me a question and I'll answer."

"What's your favorite color?" I ask, turning my head so I'm facing the TV; four teenagers are riding a formidable roller coaster that I'm pretty sure is going to jump the track any minute.

"Charcoal," he says, laughing in one quick exhale. Another shoulder kiss; I focus harder on the thrill ride on-screen.

"Do you like roller coasters?"

"Uh . . . no," he says. "Not my thing. Do you?"

"I love them," I say, raising my chin at the TV so Joel will look. The coaster in the movie is barreling through turn after turn. "That looks like the Screamer. I once rode it fourteen times in a row with my sister." I smile at the memory. Teddy doesn't do roller coasters, but Natalie and I both love them.

"When I was six, my cousins were a lot bigger than me and they threatened to pants me in front of the entire amusement park if I didn't go on the roller coaster with them," Joel says.

"Did you do it?" I ask, looking at him now, smirking.

"I did," he says, fighting a smile. "Then I aimed in their direction when I hurled afterward."

"Classy," I say, laughing. Joel looks amused, like he might laugh, but he doesn't. "Are you close to them? Your cousins?"

"Yeah." He leans back into the couch, still holding on to my arm. Like he's growing bored of talking, he starts tracing patterns on the inside of my forearm with his fingertips. Wanting to keep the conversation going, I ask something big.

"Do you know where your dad is?"

Joel shakes his head. "He used to live in Phoenix, but I haven't heard from him in a while."

"I'm sorry." I lean on his shoulder.

"Don't be," he says. "He's a total asshole. Some people shouldn't be parents, and he's one of those people." We're both quiet for a minute, me thinking of my next line of questioning since this is clearly a sore subject. But then he adds, "He used to put me in the basement."

"What do you mean?"

"He'd drag my little baby cage thing down to the basement and leave me there," he says, like he's telling me how he solved a math problem. "He'd turn up his music so he couldn't hear me crying."

"Do you *remember* that?" I ask. It reminds me of how decent my own father is—how he's called me a couple times since the funeral just to check in. I feel guilty for not giving him more of my attention.

"Yeah, a little," Joel says about the memory, dropping my hand and wiping his palms on his jeans. "I mean he didn't leave until I was almost five, so yeah. . . ."

"That's child ab—"

"Let's talk about something else," Joel cuts me off, grabbing my hand again, but this time, his grip is a little harder—a little more desperate. He glances at me and I see pain in his eyes. I jump to a lighter topic.

"Which class do you hate most?"

"English," he says automatically. He looks relieved.

"Why?"

"Too much writing."

I laugh a little, then go on. "If you could only listen to one band for the rest of your life, what would it be?" I scoot closer to him, anticipating his answer.

"Electric Freakshow, no contest," he says quickly. "In ninth grade I tried to teach myself how to play guitar, just so I could play their songs. I've been to eleven of their shows already."

"I love them too," I say. "But I've only seen them three times."

Joel looks at me again, pain gone, gleam returned. "Let's go together," he says. "They're playing a show around Thanksgiving."

I want to point out that going to the city together means being seen in public together, but I don't want to spoil the moment. Instead I nod in agreement.

I lean in close, inhaling Joel. He let me in a little, and there's nothing sexier than feeling emotionally closer to a guy you think is physically perfect. It's almost ten, but I don't care. Just before I touch Joel's lips with mine, I whisper, "Can't wait."

ELEVEN

GO

Friday at school doesn't give me the warm and fuzzies, but it's bearable since Miss Severity—whose name is Tricia—seems to have moved on from her unbridled hatred for me. Of course no one is lining up to be my friend, so I'm guessing she's put out a hit on me or something. I don't know why she won't just leave me alone—I already have enough people who hate me.

Lunch is lonely, but I spend it texting with Chris since he's done for the day and harassing me. TOMORROW. MY PLACE. CAGE MATCH, he writes.

I can't help but smile. Then, self-conscious, I dart my eyes around the cafeteria even though I know no one can see his message. To be honest, my arm is still a little sore from our play fighting the other night, but I don't want to tell him that. Instead I type:

MAYBE DINNER INSTEAD?

SURE. HOW ABOUT . . . CHICKEN????

I laugh, liking how he saw right through me. I'M GOING
BACK TO MY STERILE LEARNING ENVIRONMENT NOW, I
text. CALL ME LATER.

I HAVE A THING TONIGHT, BUT I'LL DEFINITELY CALL
YOU AFTER. OKAY?

A thing? There's a weird twist in my stomach as I type
back OKAY—maybe because it's a Friday night and Chris was
very nonspecific. Then again, it's not like he's my boyfriend.
Hell, we haven't even kissed yet. If he wants to go do . . . things,
he's allowed. I swallow hard and slide my phone into the front
pocket of my backpack.

I'm a little confused as I unwrap my sandwich, but then
I notice someone standing at the edge of my lunch table. Oh,
dear God, it's Varsity Jacket—er, Aaron. I think. How long has
he been waiting there?

"Caroline, right?" he asks, all perfect teeth and Proactiv
skin. I nod, checking behind him to make sure Tricia isn't
watching in some twisted joke. When I don't spot her at their
table, I relax slightly.

"Sorry," Aaron says. "A few of the guys sent me over. They
want to know if you have a boyfriend, and since I'm the only
one who has a class with you . . ." He shoves his hands into his
pockets, looking so embarrassed that I decide he's not messing with me.

"I do," I tell him, even though Chris is too busy doing *things* to be my boyfriend. "Sorry."

"No worries. But I'm sure the girls will be happy to hear it." He smiles, masking disappointment. I wonder if it was really "the guys" who sent him over or if he sent himself.

"See you around," he says. With a wave that I awkwardly return, Aaron leaves to join a table of red-jacket-and-jersey-wearing jocks on the other side of the room. I watch as they talk, a few looking over, and then I exhale, thinking that whether it's Aaron who likes me or someone else, I'm lucky that my Chris cover held up.

It's then that I notice Tricia standing in the cafeteria door-way in her full cheerleading uniform—which somehow makes her more terrifying as she stares daggers in my direction. I realize by her expression that I'm not off the hook at all, and I look away, unable to hold her gaze.

Chris meets me for dinner on Saturday night at Jade Palace, a tiny Chinese restaurant off campus. We're in a cozy corner booth, picking from a massive plate of orange chicken. I'm elated that it's the weekend and that I made it through Friday unscathed by Miss Severity. But I'm worried about what the rest of the year will bring.

"I wish I never switched schools," I say, glancing across the table at Chris. He's wearing a backwards hat, which is boyish and adorable, the amber light from the candle playing off his features. I've been having a hard time looking at my reflection lately, so I'm makeup free, rocking jeans and a ponytail. The best I could do was put on gloss, but it's long gone thanks to the sticky sauce.

"I'm sorry your school sucks," Chris says, trickling some soy sauce onto the plate of steamed rice. "Anything I can do?"

I shrug. "Don't think so. Although your fighting moves might come in handy with the way the first week went."

"That girl still giving you a hard time?" he asks.

I nod. "Well, I did accidentally grope her boyfriend." Chris smirks, letting it go without comment—even though he already offered several jokes earlier. "But the guy Aaron," I say. "He's making it worse. Yesterday he showed up at my lunch table and asked if I had a boyfriend, and of course Tricia was standing in the doorway like one of Satan's cheerleaders, probably thinking I was hitting on him or something."

Chris pauses midbite and lowers his chopsticks. "What'd you say?"

"Nothing. She was across the room."

He smiles. "No, what did you say when he asked if you had a boyfriend?"

I fumble with my food, trying not to appear so guilty. "I said yes." The silence carries on so long, I have to look up. Chris is waiting.

"Are you asking me out, Caroline?"

"No." Then, when I see his grin, "Maybe."

I'm burning up with embarrassment and take a shaky sip from my Diet Pepsi to avoid looking at Chris. I glance around at the other tables, but none of the customers seem even slightly interested in my humiliation. *Why did I tell him that stupid story?*

"Since you're already telling all your friends," he says nonchalantly, "I'll be your boyfriend, Caroline."

"Don't do me any favors," I mumble.

Chris reaches across the table to take my hand, carefully removing the chopsticks first. He brings my fingers to his mouth, hiding his words as he speaks, his lips brushing against my skin in soft kisses as he talks. "Let me rephrase, then," he says quietly. "I *want* to be your boyfriend."

The joking is gone, and I see in his eyes a vulnerability I don't really understand, even though I think I feel it too. My heart thumps, and when Chris lets go of my hand, tilting his head as if unsure of my answer, I shrug.

"Yeah, okay."

He bites back his smile. "I should probably warn you," he says, passing me my chopsticks. "I'm going to do super-romantic shit all the time. I'll even sing to you every night."

"Please don't."

"I'm a music major," he says. "What am I supposed to do with all this talent—take business courses?"

"Are you seriously a music major?" I ask. I should have guessed that he wouldn't be into anything boring.

Chris nods, seeming content to talk about the finer points of what a concentration in music consists of. "I play three instruments," he says between bites of chicken. "Piano, drums, and guitar—which is my favorite, obviously. But my course load includes classes like music appreciation. Which, above all else, makes you hate music—appreciatively. Doesn't really matter, though. I could go on to conduct the New York Philharmonic and my parents would still think it's a worthless degree."

"They're not big music fans?" I ask, leaning in, utterly riveted by this other side of him.

"They're older," he says. "My dad's a doctor, retired last year. Mom's a former guidance counselor. My folks travel a lot, though." He pauses. "So it's probably good I'm an only child. Less to claim at customs."

He takes a quick sip of his drink, and I feel my smile fade. It strikes me that Chris is alone. And even though lately I've felt the same way, I know that I have Teddy and, God help me—even Natalie.

"Are they gone all the time?" I ask.

"Pretty much. I'm used to it, though," he says with a wave of his hand. "I'm not sure I can remember the last holiday we spent at my house." He smiles. "My mom likes the Bahamas. I prefer Europe, but now I just stick around school." He exhales. "They think music is unstable and that I'm wasting my time. I guess they hoped I'd be a doctor or something. Turns out, I'm just too ridiculously talented. They're devastated."

"Looks and talent?" I say, trying to make him smile again. "I must be the luckiest girlfriend alive."

Chris's eyes meet mine, narrowing slightly as he looks me over. After a second he laughs to himself and tosses his napkin on the table. "Smart-ass. You know it makes me completely crazy for you, right?"

"Hey, whatever works."

A lady with short black hair and a bright blue embroidered shirt comes by to drop off the check with a couple of fortune cookies before heading off to the other tables.

"So what are your Halloween plans for next week?" Chris asks me as he throws some cash down on the table. "I could be persuaded to wear a couple's costume and win some contests if you're game."

"Uh, thanks, but I'd rather not be the rear of your jackass costume. Besides, I have to go hang with my friend Simone. We do a lame haunted house thing—it's tradition."

"Can I come?" Chris asks quietly, sliding a cookie in my direction. I take it, scrunching my forehead as I think it over. I'm unsettled and suddenly shy about him meeting my friends—and he's right (again). It's a hell of a thrill.

"Well, you did ask to be my boyfriend, so I guess that's one of the perks," I say.

"One of many, I hope," Chris says with a laugh. He climbs out of the booth, grabbing my coat to help me put it on. In the second that we're standing there, close and tangled in outerwear, I wonder why he hasn't tried to kiss me yet. Hell, I'm starting to wonder if he ever will.

When we get out the front door, heading toward my car, Chris pauses to button the top of my coat. "It's cold," he says in a quiet voice. The gesture is sweet, intimate. I smile and take him by the pockets of his hoodie to keep him close. And then he leans in to kiss me.

His lips are maddeningly gentle, barely brushing mine as his hand glides down my neck, sending chills over my entire body. I get up on my tiptoes, but just as I drape my arms over his shoulders, I feel his phone vibrate in his pocket.

"Not answering it," he murmurs into the kiss. I laugh and pull back. The phone continues to vibrate, and eventually he groans and pulls it out of his pocket.

"Yeah?" he asks into the receiver. Chris turns slightly, and my arms fall from around him. He angles his body away as he talks quietly into the phone, and I feel like I'm intruding on his conversation. I take a few steps in the direction of my car, giving him space, but Chris furrows his brow, pointing at me. "Wait," he says. Then into the phone, "No, Maria, not you."

My stomach sinks. *Maria? The same Maria he was going to see that night I gave him my number?* I don't ask. I swallow hard, wondering if I should just walk myself to my car. Chris begins to realize that I'm uncomfortable.

"I don't think so," he says for his part of the telephone conversation, but I'm ready to go home. I start to walk past him, but Chris catches the bottom of my coat, and I turn and force a smile.

"We'll talk later," I say, my voice higher pitched than usual. Chris shakes his head, telling me to wait, but I'm already moving down the sidewalk. I don't want him to explain. And I don't want to have to listen.

As I cross the parking lot, my phone buzzes. Reluctantly I check the message. I ONLY HAVE EYES FOR CAROLINE.

I pause, biting on my thumbnail as I read it three more times. YOU SURE? I write back, surprised that I'd even ask. What if he says no? How would I react to that?

POSITIVE. SHE'S THE SEXY ROBIN TO MY BATMAN.

I laugh, the tension in my shoulders relaxing. I was over-reacting. I was running. I'll have to learn to stop doing that. OMG, I write back. WE'RE NOT DRESSING AS BATMAN AND ROBIN FOR HALLOWEEN.

WE'LL SEE.

TWELVE

STAY

Back at school, I start to wonder if I'm crazy and I've conjured up a fake relationship between me and Joel—that's how much he seems to have forgotten our Friday . . . whatever it was. For three days, I try to mind control him into dropping me a note to meet him in the auditorium or merely looking at me over his shoulder in English and acknowledging that I exist. But I get an F in telekinesis—it doesn't work. My humiliation grows and by Wednesday, I'm feeling desperate and sickened at myself for letting a guy get under my skin.

"The boy's got issues," Simone says as we roam the aisle of a strip mall costume shop over the lunch period. It's Halloween, and as is tradition, we're picking over the carcasses of unwanted costumes and accessories to piece together something worthy. Normally this and the turkey races just before

Thanksgiving are the bright spots on my fall calendar, but thanks to Joel, I've lost my spirit.

"Can I put a moratorium on speaking his name?" I ask, fingering a feather boa.

"You got it," she says. She's sucking on a Blow Pop, occasionally crunching as she bites a piece off. She crunches for a whole aisle, then says, "He probably has some weird abandonment hangup and you didn't pay enough attention to him."

"Did you go deaf?" I ask. "Or do you just have short-term memory loss?"

She turns on her heels to face me; her shoes squeak on the linoleum. "Linus. I'll kick him in the shins for you—if that would make it better." She picks up a toy tommy gun. "Hell, I'll put a hit out on him if you want me to." I laugh weakly and start walking again. From behind me, she gets to the point. "All I'm saying is that since he happens to be monopolizing your brain space, we might as well talk it out."

"Maybe he's just not into me anymore," I say sadly, giving in. I pick up a torn open package of fake mustaches and put one on, turning to Simone. "I can find someone else, right?" I ask.

"A gentleman like you? Absolutely." She smiles and grabs a bonnet from an oversize baby costume, putting it over her hair. "You just need to stop being a child about all of it." She waggles the pacifier at me and then tosses the costume back onto the shelf. "This isn't the 1800s. A girl doesn't have to wait around for a guy to text. If you want to talk to Joel about his continued romantic flakiness, take control of your life and ask him." She looks at me in that reality-check sort of way, and I reach to pull off my mustache and shrug.

"You know they didn't have cell phones in the 1800s, right?" I say.

"Doesn't mean you have to be as clueless."

I laugh for real and finally notice part of a costume that might actually work. As I pull it from the shelf, I think that Simone's right. Passivity isn't doing me any favors.

I stuff the costume and accessories into my hand basket and turn to my friend. "I'm going to tell Joel that this hot-and-cold crap doesn't work for me," I say, sounding resolved.

"There's my girl," she says, grabbing a homecoming sash and a plastic machete. She inspects the fake blade, and I take out my phone and scroll as I walk toward the registers with my items. I find Joel's number and write:

I'M OVER IT. Maybe not the most eloquent speech I've ever given, but when I hit send, I don't regret it. Even though deep down, I know I'm not nearly as *over* him as I wish I were.

I plunk my basket on the counter, and then Simone is next to me asking if the fake blood in a package will stain her skin. When Joel's return text pops up, there's a leap in my chest, a guarded hope, and I turn to smile at Simone, holding it up for her to see.

I'M NOT.

After school, I hurry home and drop my bag in the entryway, then grab an apple from the kitchen and head upstairs.

"Mom?" I call, but she doesn't answer. "Mom?"

No one seems to be home, so I go to my room and take off my school clothes. Simone and I split up to check in at our respective houses and change into costumes—we're going to watch a scary movie at her place, then hit the haunted house at the community center. But fresh off an afternoon of cute text exchanges with Joel—he can't wait to draw me again, he can't wait to kiss me—I'm planning on stopping by his place to invite him along. I want to spend time with him, but also, as I look at myself in my gingham dress, red shoes, cape, and mask, I can admit that I want him to see me in my costume. Superhero Dorothy is awesome.

I can't help but smile as I spritz a little perfume on my wrists, imagining Joel kissing them again. Feeling like it's something that Dorothy might wear, I take Gram's necklace from its white box I have stashed in my closet and put it on. When I see the N resting against my skin, I'm filled with comfort, ready to make this Halloween unforgettable. Ready to spend my first Halloween with Joel Ryder.

Twenty minutes later, nerves are mingled with excitement as I turn onto Joel's street. I park a couple houses down from his so I can check for lipstick smudges on my teeth without him seeing me. I climb out of the car, shivering a little: Fall always seems to change to winter on Halloween, even though it's seemed colder than usual since . . . I stop, a wave of sadness washing over me. It's been cold since Gram died.

I'm still thinking about Gram as I make my way down the sidewalk, touching absently at the necklace, and it isn't until I'm right in front of Joel's house that I glance up.

I freeze.

Lauren is standing on Joel's porch while he stands in the doorway, his hand on her arm. Her long, wavy dark hair is unmistakable. The moment is intimate. And when they embrace, the moment is heartbreaking. I want to sink straight into the ground and disappear, but then Joel glances over Lauren's shoulder to see me standing there. In a superhero mask and sparkly red shoes. His eyes widen, and I expect him to call to me. To walk past his ex-girlfriend and invite me in.

But instead our gazes just lock, and after what feels like forever, but is probably less than fifteen seconds, I force myself to turn around and leave, rushing to the car before Lauren can see me running off with my cape between my legs. I'm humiliated. Hurt.

And the minute I pull away from his house, I take out my phone to send him one last text at the stoplight. LEAVE ME ALONE, I write. And then I turn it off so I won't have to see his reply.

TWELVE

GO

I'm panicked, rushing toward the college center as my bright green boots clop on the pavement. I hear several snickers, but more whistles, as I pass people walking around campus, but I ignore them. After all, I am dressed as Sexy Robin—which, if I wasn't so worried, would be completely humiliating. Actually, it's still really humiliating. I yank open the heavy glass door of the building and nearly kill myself on the slippery tile floor as I get inside.

About twenty minutes before he was supposed to pick me up, Chris called me at my dad's house from the infirmary. Turns out that my boyfriend had been too impatient to wait for the elevator and decided to take the stairs—at bat speed. He fell down the last flight, injuring his leg. If he's okay, I'm going to kill him.

"I'm looking for Christopher Drake?" I say to the girl

behind the information desk. She looks up and then presses her lips together to hide her smile.

"I'm guessing he's Batman?"

Seriously going to kill him. "Yep." My costume consists of knee-high green boots and a green sequin skirt with a red bustier. I'm wearing a denim jacket, but still, it's over the top. Simone helped me order it online, and when I first put it on, I nearly covered myself with a blanket. Simone swore it didn't look trashy—just "cutely sexy." Judging from the looks I got jogging through campus, I'm not sure she was telling me the truth.

I thank the girl at the desk after she gives me directions. Before I walk away, I ask, "So . . . he's okay, right?" She takes a while to answer, and I feel my entire body sway with worry.

"I'm not sure," she says, glancing at her computer, then back at me. She must tell from my expression that I'm not exactly taking this well. She reaches to put a warm hand on my arm. "Hey," she says soothingly. "I'm sure he's fine. If not, they would have sent him to the ER."

That's true. I nod, thanking her, and then let my heart settle down. I can't always expect the worst. This isn't like with Gram. It doesn't always end in tragedy.

I walk inside the large room with paper-covered exam tables. There are several people in varying degrees of injury.

One guy is moaning, clutching his stomach. Another one has an ice pack over his face. Halloween on campus—it'll probably only get crazier as the night goes on. It doesn't take me long to find Chris, laid up with his foot wrapped in Ace bandages. At that moment he looks over, his eyes a little glassy from what I guess are painkillers, and smiles.

"You are certainly a sexy Robin," he says in a raspy voice.

I bite back my laugh and start toward him, the clicking of my heels drawing the stares of several other patients. "Don't you dare be funny until you tell me you're all right," I say, stopping at this side. He's still wearing a muscled Batman chest plate, a bright yellow belt.

"Yeah," he says. "I'm fine." Chris lets his head fall back. "Although I really did have my heart set on sweeping the costume contest circuit." Even now, looking completely pathetic and sorry, Chris makes light of things. I wonder if he'll always do that—even when things aren't so funny. I reach to brush his blond hair to the side, and he closes his eyes. I want to lean down and kiss him better, relieved he's okay. But instead I just sigh.

"Does it hurt?" I ask, motioning to his leg.

"Right now? No." He sits up, looking pretty dazed. "Hairline fracture near the ankle. No treatment but to stay off it for a few weeks."

That doesn't sound like fun, but at least he's not in the

hospital. At that thought, I swallow hard and force a smile. "So can you go home?" I ask him. I exhale when he says yes and calls for the nurse.

I open Chris's door for him as he crutches in. Looking away, I drop his prescription on his desk while he changes. When I turn around, he's shirtless in a pair of basketball shorts. I can't deny that my pulse quickens: He's incredible.

I watch as he hops over to ease into bed, wincing a few times as he settles under the sheets. When he's done, he looks in my direction.

"Come cuddle with me," he murmurs, although his tone leads me to believe that isn't exactly what he's thinking. "Come love me, Caroline."

"Are you sure you're even injured?"

"Mm-hmm."

"Stop being cute," I say, slipping out of my jacket and boots before joining him. Chris puts the blanket over my shoulders, taking me by the waist to turn me toward him. He slides his knee between mine. My costume is uncomfortably tight, but the heat of Chris's skin is intoxicating. I curl up next to him, comfortable—not pressured or anxious.

"I'm sorry I ruined Halloween," he whispers. "I'll make it up to you next year."

Next year. "Deal," I say, not acknowledging that would

imply we'll still be together in a year. Chris shifts, his every movement making me a little crazier. His hand grazes my hip, and finally I can't handle it anymore.

I take his arm and pull him closer—sliding underneath him as he adjusts. Chris pauses, looking me over like he's surprised that we're in such a compromising position. But my heart is racing and my body is tingling. I reach to put my hand on his chest and feel his heart pounding, too. He rests on his elbow, coming incredibly close to me as he brushes back my hair.

"Christopher," I murmur when he doesn't make a move. "Just kiss me."

"I don't want to ruin this," he says more seriously than I'd ever expect him to be capable of.

Does he not see how nuts I am for him? Before I can rethink it, I lift my head to kiss him. He tastes like candy and boy and something so right I can't even put it into words. As he deepens the kiss, I make a soft sound and Chris pulls back with a wicked grin. "You're fun," he murmurs. When I laugh, he carefully flips us over to take the pressure off his leg. I kiss him again until we both can hardly breathe.

I'm not sure how long we spend kissing, but it's not until I hear my phone buzzing across the room that I glance at the clock. It's gotten really late.

I straighten and stare down at Chris as he reaches for my Robin belt buckle to pull me back to him.

"Are you going to try and get me naked now?" I ask with a smirk.

"I'm still playing hard to get," he says. When I don't budge, he sits up and kisses low on my neck. Then he leans back to look at me. "Unless, of course, you want to get naked."

"I was supposed to be home an hour ago." I give him a quick peck. "Ask me again next time."

"Uh, I believe you're the one who asked."

"True. Well, then, I'll ask again next time." I kiss him once more before climbing up, smoothing down my ridiculous costume.

I grab my things and zip up my boots, looking over my shoulder to see Chris blinking slowly like he's falling asleep.

"You better call me," he says as if he's a one-night stand I'm walking out on.

"I would," I say teasingly, "but I'll probably be too busy making out with strange boys on park benches."

He chuckles. "Guess I was wrong about you."

I walk back over and lean down to give him a slow, sweet kiss good night. I practically have to drag myself from the comfort of his arms, the safety I feel when I'm with him.

I'm so happy—so not myself as I climb into the elevator. I can't stop smiling, laughing to myself like I've gone completely mad. And as I cross the lobby, I realize why: I'm pretty sure I've fallen in love with Christopher Drake.

THIRTEEN

STAY

Enraged, hurt, and humiliated by Joel—*he just* stood *there with Lauren!*—I drive in the rain without thinking to the place I feel safest. I end up parked in front of Gram's. *You'll help me figure it out*, I think to her. And then I remember that she's dead.

And this time, for the first time, I cry.

In her driveway, my tears soak the superhero mask until I rip it off and toss it onto the seat next to me. I cry for every second that I haven't since Gram died nearly three weeks ago. I cry for her. I cry for Joel. I cry for everything.

When the car windows fog up from my outburst, I get out and go inside. I'm shocked by the emptiness of the place, how barren it looks with all of Gram's stuff gone—not in boxes, but actually gone. I guess I hadn't thought about what it'd look like without her possessions. But what it looks like is nothing.

Bare floors. Naked walls. Discolored spots where things sat or hung for years.

In the isolating quiet, I turn on my phone, intending to call Simone, but see that I have four texts and two missed calls from Joel. I read the texts:

CAROLINE, SERIOUSLY, THAT WAS NOT WHAT YOU THINK.

I'M AT YOUR HOUSE; WHERE ARE YOU?

I'M WAITING FOR YOU HERE. I HOPE YOUR MOM DOESN'T CALL THE COPS ON ME.

TEXT ME. PLEASE.

In my hand, the phone rings again. "Aren't we persistent today?" I ask bitterly.

"Finally," Joel says, sounding relieved. "Why'd you take off like that? I texted you right away—and I tried to follow you, but you were NASCAR driving out of my neighborhood."

I'm not in the mood for jokes. "I wasn't about to stick around and see you and Lauren defaulting on your breakup."

"Defaulting?" He laughs. It's such a rarity from him that for a moment, my insides soften. But then I remember feeling humiliated. I don't respond.

"Listen, Caroline. I'm sorry, but it's not what you think. And if you give me five minutes to explain, you'll see that I'm not the bad guy here."

Then why does it feel like you are?

When I'm quiet, he keeps talking. "Where are you right now? I want to see you. You know I don't like talking on the phone."

"At my grandmother's," I admit. I walk over and open the front door, then step outside. "Where are you parked?" I ask, looking in the direction of my mom's house.

"Right across from . . . Oh, I see you. Okay, I'm coming over."

I don't say good-bye: I just end the call. Then, instead of waiting on the porch like an advertisement for neediness, I turn and walk inside, leaving the door wide open behind me. When I hear the floorboards creak, I turn and see Joel. He doesn't look sorry. He just looks sort of amused.

"Nice outfit," he says, his dark eyes sparkling. I cross my arms over my chest in response. He nods, getting that I'm not backing down.

"I owe you an explanation," he says. "It's not what you think. Lauren was having a thing with a friend." He pauses; I stare. "Okay, yeah, she's not thrilled about the breakup. She wants to get back together."

I grip my arms tighter.

"But we're *not*," Joel says quickly. I like how much he talks when I don't—I'll have to stay quiet more often. "I told her that. I told her that we're done for good. I like someone else."

"Joel," I say harshly. "After Friday night at your house,

you basically ignored me at school. Maybe you're not getting back together with Lauren, but you aren't exactly with me, either. At least not in public."

"You know why I don't want to put things out there just yet," he says, raising his voice. "It's too new, and I just ended things with Lauren. People would—"

"What?" I snap. "What would people do? God, Joel, why do you care anyway? Unless you're lying about what I saw today—unless things aren't over with her."

"I told you Lauren and I are done and we're done," he says defensively. Then he takes a deep breath. "I don't want to hurt her. She's still into me and this," he says, waving his hand between us, "would hurt her. I may not want to be with her, but I don't want to wreck her either. Surely you can understand that."

I can, but I don't say it. I'm so confused, and being here at Gram's makes me think about her, her words.

Be careful who you love, Caroline. Never let them take too much. Is this what she meant? Because right now, raw and hurt, I think that maybe I am in love with Joel—but it's nothing like I thought it would be. It's insecurity and heartache, disappointment tempered with the occasional high. If I don't stop it . . . I wonder if he'll somehow wreck me, just the way he says he doesn't want to wreck Lauren.

"You have to go," I tell Joel suddenly, trying to channel

Super-Dorothy. "I need time to think . . . and I can't do that with you staring at me." I push past him and head toward the front door. Joel walks out after me, and when he's on the porch, I lock up the house.

"Caroline," he says, touching my arm. And I realize it's the same way he was touching Lauren's. I brush him off and hurry down the stairs, processing the fact that I'm dissing the guy I've liked my whole life. But I need to decide whether I believe what he said about what happened with Lauren. And then I need to decide just how much longer I'm willing to be his secret.

I don't feel like I can go home—not with tear-streaked cheeks and an inquisitive mother—so I drive. I end up in the grocery store parking lot. It looks like a scene from an apocalypse movie: only a few cars, dim streetlights, and zombies limping by.

Crying has messed with me, leaving me empty. I almost wish I could bottle it back up, but the damage has been done. When I reach up to grip Gram's charm, my eyes widen and I scratch myself, feeling around for it. It's gone. I grab the rearview mirror to check, and sure enough, the necklace that I so desperately wanted, that I lied to my sister for, is missing. I burst out crying once again; I'm in free fall—broken and lonely, sitting by myself on Halloween at a grocery store of all places.

My tears only stop when my phone buzzes. I see it's Simone but ignore her, even as she continues to text, asking where I am. And when I read BE SURE TO GIVE LOVER BOY A KISS FOR ME, I turn my phone off altogether. Going home is even less an option now, not when my sister is there and I lost the necklace she's been frantically searching for. I can't go to Joel's, and I don't have the energy to explain to Simone what happened. I want to start over where no one knows me.

A sad smile crosses my lips as I realize where I can go. I shift into gear and get on the highway. Once I'm cruising at sixty-five, I plug in the Joel mix I made long before he first kissed me, the one filled with hopeful instead of toxic songs. I sing at the top of my lungs as I fly down the road, thinking not of Joel, but of someone else I haven't met yet—someone who'll make me feel lighter and better instead of like the worst version of myself.

Thirty minutes later I'm parking in front of a two-story house with white siding and black shutters. I check the mirror, and thankfully, my face is almost back to normal. There's a group of little kids—ghosts and princesses—scrambling away from the doorway. I start up the front steps and ring the bell, taking a deep breath and then another just before the front door opens.

"Trick or treat," I say, smiling. "I hope it's okay that I'm here."

My dad looks absolutely stunned to see me, but his face breaks with a huge smile. "There's never been a better surprise," he says, stepping back to wave me inside.

I only stay an hour, long enough to get the tour and chat with Debra about her latest decorating ideas for the spare room. It's nothing groundbreaking, but it is a nice distraction. In a way, it almost feels like the start of something better. I leave with my confidence, though frayed, returned slightly. At least enough to know that I no longer want to be Joel Ryder's on-the-side girl. Had I known that just an hour with my dad could bring me even a little bit of clarity, I might have stopped by sooner.

THIRTEEN

GO

I spend the rest of the weekend helping my stepmother devour the leftover Halloween candy. She made caramel apples, but I told her I had to draw the line somewhere—and it was after a bag of M&M's, a full-size Snickers, and a handful of candy corn. Then I thought better of it and grabbed an apple anyway.

"Maybe you can bring one over to your mom's," she says quietly from across the kitchen table. "Tell her you made it."

I smile at Debbie. "First of all," I say, "my mother would know on sight that I didn't—she's well aware that I can't make anything that doesn't come with a packet of powdered cheese. And second of all, I think you're just trying to make me go see my mom."

"I am," she admits. She leans forward on her elbows, smiling softly. I think then about how much I like talking with her—almost like an older sister. My stomach clenches when I think of Natalie at my mother's house—keeping me out.

"I'm not on the best of terms with Natalie," I say. "Maybe when she finally moves out, I'll go by there." Debbie tsks at the answer.

"I never had any siblings, Caroline, so I'm not really speaking from experience. But I promise you, there will come a day when you really need someone—and it'd be nice to have a sister. Everyone needs family."

"It's my family who doesn't need me," I murmur, and stand from the table. I thank Debbie again for the apple before heading up to my room. My stepmother's words stick with me, though, so when I sit on my bed, I send my mother a text.

HOPE YOU HAD A NICE HALLOWEEN, MOM. I exhale, just this simple act making me feel a little less like the worst daughter in the world. Since I'm on a roll, I even text Teddy.

HEY. SEE YOU TOMORROW AT SUNDAY DINNER?

OF COURSE, he responds right away. DORM FOOD IS PRACTICALLY POISONOUS. BTW, PHIL IS JOINING US.

FANTASTIC. BE SURE TO TELL HIM TO ACT CIVILIZED.

CAN'T PROMISE ANYTHING.

I help Debbie set the table Sunday evening, a comfortableness at home that I haven't felt since living with Gram. I'm not sure when my temporary exile turned into an actual life, but I decide not to question it. Not when I'm finally starting to feel like myself.

About twenty minutes later, my father is upstairs looking for a book he's been meaning to give my brother, and Teddy comes in with Phil in tow. Just to break my chops, Phil is wearing a button-up shirt with a bow tie (where did he even get that?), and his hair is slick and brushed dramatically to the side. I half expect him to pull out a monocle.

"My lady," he says with a bow when he sees me. I swat his shoulder and walk past, rolling my eyes at my brother.

"This is his version of civilized," he says.

"Oh, Phillip," Debbie says, putting her hand on her hip as she watches from the kitchen. "You look adorable."

Phil grins, then goes to help my stepmother carry food to the table. Teddy catches my eye and motions to the other room like he has to talk to me in private. I furrow my brow but follow him. I hope this doesn't have to do with our mom.

"Your friend is entirely unbalanced," I say the minute we're in the living room.

"I know. That's why we love him, though." My brother fidgets in that way he does when he's hiding something. Teddy's skills at secret keeping are nonexistent, and just like always, my stomach knots as I wait for the news to drop.

"What is it?" I ask.

"I brought you a present."

I fight back my smile. "You did? Why?"

He scoffs. "Just say thank you, Coco." He holds out a small white box, and I take it with a suspicious look. When I open it, my eyes immediately fill with tears.

"How . . . Teddy, how did you know?" Pain and happiness fill my chest, and I blubber out a few breathless thank-yous.

My brother nods, his brown eyes getting misty. "I was helping Natalie the other weekend with some of Gram's things, and when I saw it, I knew you'd want it. And I think Gram would want you to have it."

With the mixture of a cry and a laugh I crush my brother to me. Between us in the small white box is a piece of my life that is gone. It's my grandmother's initial necklace—something I'd forgotten about until this moment. And now it's mine.

"So, Caroline," my dad starts as we sit down to dinner. "Debbie and I were wondering about your plans for Thanksgiving." The entire table seems to shift with discomfort at his question.

I swallow hard, trying to draw some strength from the initial necklace I'm wearing, the metal cool where it rests near my throat. "I thought I'd stay here," I reply.

Everyone is silent for a long moment, and I'm sure I'm not imagining the weight of my brother's stare from across the table. I'd almost rather talk about anything else right now.

Hell, I'd even bring up Chris just for a chance to change the subject. But I don't get off the hook that easily.

"Although we'd love that," my father says softly, "I think your mother is expecting you there for the holiday. Your aunt Claudia will be in town, and Teddy is going over—"

"And me," Phil adds nonchalantly before taking a big bite from his roll. I look up to see my dad watching me.

"Yes, and Phillip will be there. Anyway"—he presses his lips into a smile—"I really think you should go, Caroline. I think you have to."

I lower my eyes. "You're forcing me?" I say it weakly, but I'm feeling panicked. There's a clink as Teddy sets down his fork.

"We'll all be there, Coco," my brother says. "And it's time. Mom needs you, and . . ." He stops, and when I look up, his expression is pleading. "Just say you'll go."

I look at Debbie. She's Switzerland: her face pleasant and nonjudging. That's when finally I nod. I don't promise to go—I don't say it aloud. But it's a silent agreement—with my mother, with my family. I know that Natalie and I have a lot of unfinished business. And as I excuse myself from the table the minute we're done eating, I hope that the fallout with my sister won't be big enough to ruin Thanksgiving for everyone.

FOURTEEN

STAY

When I wanted Joel's attention, I never got it; now that I don't want it, all he does is text me. I spend the week after Halloween ignoring him, deleting messages like I MISS YOU and SERIOUSLY, CALL ME. Because really, how much could he miss me—we weren't together that often. And somehow the fact that he hasn't actually called himself—just texted to tell me to call him—leaves a bad taste in my mouth.

So instead of dialing, I focus on other things.

"What are we doing tonight?" I ask Simone as we walk out of school on Friday. "I've got to get out of here. Not that I'm obsessing, but there are *strangers* in Gram's house right now, possibly buying it."

"Oh, Linus, I forgot about that," Simone says. "I'm so sorry."

"Thanks. So how can we keep my mind off of the fact that

my home is being ripped out from under me; oh, and that Joel is a wishy-washy man whore too?"

Simone checks her phone. "Party?" she asks. "There's one at Angel's tonight."

"Sure," I say, shrugging, knowing that at the very least, Angel has videogames and I can wipe the floor with anyone who challenges me to All-Stars Racing. And also knowing that in seventh grade, Angel and Joel got in a fistfight at school—there's no way my pseudo-ex will be there.

We park on an intersecting street near the back alley in case the police show up and we have to run to our car. Simone applies red lipstick to her luscious lips while I smear on balm with my pointer finger by the light of the flip-down mirror.

"Ready?" she asks, opening her door.

"Let's go."

We knock, but no one answers—the music's too loud to hear—so we just walk in. The entryway is crowded with conversations. A few people glance at us and nod or wave before diving headfirst back into noise.

"Did you tell the girls we were coming?" I ask. One second later, like they're tracking us with GPS devices, Gwen and Felicity are by our sides.

"It's about time," Felicity shouts over the bass. "Did you go for coffee in Canada or something?" She's wearing plaid pants that literally no one else on earth could pull off with a pair of black suspenders, one over her shoulder and one hanging by her side. "I need confirmation that Ryan Elgin is hot for me."

I glance at Gwen, who shakes her head no so slightly that it's barely noticeable. She looks back down at the phone in her hand, and I wonder if she'd self-destruct if she ever lost it.

"Why do you think he's into you?" Simone asks curiously. Ryan Elgin is the captain of the football team, the class president, and a Mormon. Felicity may dress ironically straight edge, but Ryan's the real deal: square as they come. There's no way he's flirting with anyone other than a God-fearing cheerleader or student council member who needs saving.

"He looked at my sisters," Felicity says, leaning in like it's a secret but still shouting so we can hear. She motions to her chest in case we didn't get the reference. A couple of guys near a tray of chips look at us . . . well, at her.

"They are quite nice, your sisters," Simone says, making Gwen laugh. "I mean, who doesn't check them out once in a while?" She wiggles her eyebrows at Felicity. "I'm just not sure. . . . I mean, you know Ryan. And his . . . beliefs."

"I think I can lure him to the dark side," Felicity says. "Come on, he's playing a game in the living room. I'll stand near him and you guys hang back and watch. See if he checks me out again."

Gwen rolls her eyes but follows Felicity; Simone grabs my hand and pulls me through the sweaty masses on the main level of the house. Once we're though the entryway and hall, we need to cut through the kitchen to get to the living room. But there's a major pileup near the refrigerator, so we're forced to stop. My eyes fall on the kitchen table, where a group of guys is playing cards.

Angel is at the head of the table, and because the universe obviously hates me . . . Joel is to his left.

Like he can feel my stare, he looks up. He leans back in his chair, eyes on me, wearing an expression I can't place. Simone sees him and squeezes my hand, then looks at me, concerned. Angel hits Joel on the arm—it's his turn. He looks down at the cards in his hands and plays one, then he leans over and says something to Angel.

Great, back to ignoring me in public.

Simone tugs at my hand—the bottleneck is gone and so are Felicity and Gwen. We're almost to the kitchen doorway when Joel stands and works his way around the table and through the crowd; before I realize what's happening, he's standing right in front of me, invading my personal space. I drop Simone's hand and stare at him. She turns her body away but stays right next to me, giving me privacy but telling me that she's here for me when I need her.

"I thought you and Angel hated each other," I say.

"Guys don't hold grudges," he says, shrugging. His voice is low—the only reason I can hear him is that he's talking right into my ear. "We're good."

"Oh," I say, "well, excuse me. You're in my way." I point toward the doorway, fully intending to follow the girls into the other room and focus my energy on gauging whether a Mormon likes a hipster.

Joel takes another step closer to me; our chests could touch if I took a deep enough breath . . . considering I'm holding it, there's little worry of that happening.

"Hey, Ryder, you still in?" someone calls from the direction of the table. I look and five pairs of eyes are on me. Joel doesn't flinch; he stares at my face.

"I'm out," he says loudly. His breath smells like mint.

"What are you doing?" I whisper, searching those dark eyes for an explanation. They're on fire tonight.

"I'm doing what you wanted," he says. "I don't want to lose you. I don't want you to be confused about us. I'm telling everyone."

He steps even closer still and puts his palms on my jaw and his lips on mine. I hear Simone suck in her breath as Joel kisses me—hard—right there in the middle of Angel Hernandez's party for the entire world to see.

I want to pull back and smack him; I want to tell him that one kiss doesn't make it all better. But it's a grand gesture like they do in movies, and it kind of *does* make it better. So instead of pulling away, I wrap my hands around his low waist and hold him tight, letting it happen. Completely in the moment, I don't think of anything else but being here . . . with him. I'm addicted to Joel, getting my fix. At least now, everyone knows he's addicted to me right back.

FOURTEEN

GO

My eyes wander to the dry-erase calendar pinned to Chris's wall; it's just two weeks until Thanksgiving. I'm on Chris's bed and he's next to me, strumming his guitar quietly, pretending not to listen as I hold the phone to my ear. My stomach is in knots—when my mother answers, I close my eyes.

"Hi, Mom," I say. She's silent for a moment, and it surprises me. I'm not sure why, but I guess I expected her to fall over herself, saying how much she misses me. When she doesn't, there's a small tug of regret. "Sorry I haven't called," I say.

"I'm sorry too," she responds softly. "Is everything okay? Are you okay?"

I lean back against the wall, and Chris adjusts the strings of his guitar instead of playing anything. He's the one who forced me to call, saying that he wouldn't come to Thanksgiving dinner with me until I told my mom about him. I didn't have the courage to tell him the entire story behind my rift with her. For all he knows, we're a little distant, my sister sucks, and my brother is the link between us. But I haven't told him about how I left Gram the night she died. I let him assume that she died before I went to the party.

"I'm good, Mom," I say. "I wanted to call you about Thanksgiving."

She seems to hold her breath and then, "Have you decided to spend it with your father?"

"No, actually," I say, "I was hoping I could come to your house." My eyes start to tear up, a weight lifted off my chest. When my mother starts talking again, I know she can feel it too.

"I'd love that, Caroline," she says. "We'd all love to have you here."

I smile and glance over at Chris, who's watching his guitar, but his lips are upturned as he eavesdrops. "Do you mind if I bring someone?"

"Of course not," she says. "Simone?"

"Well, yes, Simone. But someone else, too. His name is Christopher." Chris wrinkles his nose at the use of his full name.

"Oh." My mother sounds kind of stunned. "Uh, sure. Is he . . . a friend of yours?"

I may be blushing when I answer. "I guess. He's also my sort-of boyfriend." Chris's eyes snap up to mine when I say this, but I'm waiting for him with a smile. "Or like my real one," I correct.

"I didn't know you had a boyfriend," my mother responds quietly. "But yes, I'd love to meet him. Just promise me you'll stay for dessert. I'm making Gram's favorite—pumpkin cheesecake."

There's sorry in her words, sorry that spreads through me and injects me with her grief. Our grief. "I promise," I say, thinking that even though we're still so far apart, my mother and I have things in common, have people in common. "Mom," I say, beginning to fidget with the zipper of my hoodie. "How . . . are you?"

She doesn't hesitate. "I'm sad, Caroline. I'm just very sad."

I sniffle back the start of my tears. "Yeah. Me too." Chris reaches over to take my hand from my lap, and I appreciate that he's here. I'm glad that I can count on him . . . but not depend on him. This is my own mess to clean up.

"I'll see you soon," I say to my mother.

"Good-bye, Caroline." And for the first time since my grandmother died, I feel like I've made my mom happy. As if maybe I've changed a little, and this time for the better.

"You okay?" Chris asks. I look over and push his guitar to

the side so I can get closer to him. I lean in to kiss him, pause, and then kiss him again.

"Thanks for bullying me into calling," I murmur as he pulls me onto his lap. "And we only have about five minutes before Simone gets here."

"Then you should probably stop talking," he says, kissing my jaw, my neck. I smile and thread my fingers through his hair. It's like things are finally in place, and so I let the happiness overwhelm me until Simone is knocking on the dorm room door.

To take her mind off her latest mistake with Alan Fritz—I can't even imagine how that one happened—Simone is up visiting Clinton for the day. We're lounging on a few floor pillows, painting our nails, as Chris plays his guitar on the bed. He has yet to let me hear the song he supposedly wrote for me, but I don't totally hate it when he sings—which is surprisingly often. Especially when he's lost in his guitar. It's actually sort of sweet when he does.

His crutches are collecting dust in the corner of his room since he prefers to limp rather than actually use them. And as the minutes tick by, Simone lets out a bored exhale.

"I just don't know why I can't meet a good guy," Simone says. "It's not like I'm picking them based on looks—I actually tried to date a nice one. Turns out they're all just closet assholes."

"Every single one of them," Chris says, and grins at her. "But hey," he adds, hitting a chord off-key and then apologizing. "I know someone you might like." I dart a look to warn him not to get involved, but Simone is already smiling.

"Oh, yeah, College Christopher? What's he like?"

Chris notices my look, but we both know it's too late to back out now. Finding Simone a guy is never the problem. Finding Simone a guy who can actually live up to her standards is.

"I think he's rather handsome," Chris says. "He's a good snuggler, too. His name is Ed, and I happen to know that he's currently single. I can call him if you want to hang out."

Simone leans over and drags a long stroke of red paint across Chris's thumbnail. "Okay," she says with a small smile. "Let's see if this Ed dude can keep up."

Ed cannot keep up. After he came to meet us, the four of us headed to the dining hall to eat. Chris and I were cautiously optimistic at first, especially when Simone laughed at all of Ed's jokes. And he was definitely cute—dark longish hair, big green eyes—but by the time we head back toward the dorms, Simone's interest level seems to wane.

"You should be using your crutches," I tell Chris when he reaches to hold my hand as we cross the street. "You're going to make it worse."

"I don't want to use them," he says, glancing back to where Simone and Ed are trailing behind us. "Crutches make me look weak."

"Linus," Simone calls, pointing toward the student center. "Isn't that your brother?"

I turn and see Teddy and Phil, bundled up in scarves and hats, as they walk in our direction. Chris bumps his shoulder into mine. "Are you finally going to introduce me to your brother?" he asks. "Or am I like your shameful secret?"

"You are definitely shameful," I say, and then wave to my brother to get his attention. He offers a nod, and then he and Phil exchange a look.

"Hey, Coco," he says when he reaches us. His nose is red from the cold, and he darts an uncertain look at Chris. I say hi and then turn to Phil.

"Dork," I say.

"Loser," he returns. Simone steps away from Ed like she doesn't want anyone to think they're here together and says hi to my brother and Phil before coming to stand on the other side of me.

"Teddy," I say, touching Chris's arm. "This is Chris Drake."

Again Teddy and Phil make some telepathic comment before Teddy smiles tightly. "I know who you are," he says to Chris.

To his credit, my boyfriend only looks surprised and offers his hand. "It's nice to meet you," he says. "Your sister's told me a lot of good things about you." But there's a nervousness creeping over my neck as I watch my brother glance at Chris's hand and then turn to me.

"You're not dating him, are you?" he asks.

Simone tenses next to me, and I think Chris is too stunned to react at all. The only person doing anything is Phil, who is shaking his head like some disappointed parent.

"Teddy," I say very seriously. "Stop." I can't think of one time in my life when my brother acted like an overprotective jerk. Until now.

Teddy coughs out a disbelieving laugh. He marches over and takes my arm to lead me a few feet away before laying into me. "What the hell are you doing?"

"Uh, I'm sorry," I say, not bothering to lower my voice. "What are *you* doing? Have you lost your mind?"

"Clearly you have. This guy"—he motions toward Chris, who's turned toward us and is ghostly pale—"is a womanizer. Coco, he's probably screwed every girl on campus."

"That's not true," Chris snaps. My brother ignores him and goes on, and Phil takes a step closer in case he has to intervene. I lock eyes with Simone for a moment as she stands there, mouth gaping open. I'm not even sure where Ed is before my brother is talking again.

"You're not allowed to date him," Teddy says, shaking his head. "I know you don't like being told what to do, but I'm your brother. And I'd be a shitty one if I—"

"Teddy," Simone says soothingly, stepping in front of him and putting her hands on his chest. "Let's ease off. I think you're going to pop a vein." She shoots a panicked look in my direction, but I'm still just standing here, staring at my brother like he's gone crazy. Only now . . . I feel a little sick.

"Let's go," I say to Simone, turning away quickly, but she doesn't follow—she's trying to calm Teddy. My head is swirling with thoughts and suspicion. Everything had started to work out; it was just like fate—that's what Chris said.

I'm speed walking back to the dorm when suddenly Chris is next to me, jogging to keep up although he has to take an occasional hop to lessen the pressure on his injured leg.

"We should talk about this, Caroline," he says flatly. "Don't run away from me."

I stop short and turn to him. His eyes are wild, and I'm not sure what exactly we're doing. I don't know what to think anymore. So I just nod, my brow furrowed, and walk with him back to his room. Simone texts to tell me she's taking off and that she'll call me later to do a play-by-play on the drama.

I'm cautious, trying to keep all of the feelings out until I can sort through them. I don't want them to hurt me. I don't want to feel them.

When we get back to Chris's room, he tears off his coat and tosses it at his closet, pacing the floor like he's about to lose it. "I've never lied to you," he says suddenly, as if I've accused him. "I would never lie to you, Caroline. You know that, right?"

Do I?

"And your brother . . ." He runs his hand roughly through his hair as he considers his words. "I don't know. I don't even know him. Maybe one of the girls I dated is friends with him or something."

"Have you slept around?" I ask quietly. I'm not sure it matters, as long as he's not doing it now. But when he hesitates before answering, there's a sinking in my gut. Chris must see the change because he walks over and gathers me into a hug, resting his cheek on the top of my head.

"I know it sounds bad," he says, his breath warm in my hair. "But I'm not some player. I didn't lead them on—I'd never do that. I wasn't serious with any of those girls. I've never been serious about anyone but you. Caroline," he whispers, his fingers tickling absently up my spine as he pulls me tighter to him. There it is again, that certain way he can say my name. "My sweet Caroline."

I hug him, closing my eyes against the doubt.

"You're the only girl I want," he says. "I love you." He pulls away to laugh softly, looking surprised at this own words. His eyes are wide and vulnerable, as if a word from me can crush him. "I'm totally in love with you," he murmurs.

And although I feel it too . . . I can't bring myself to say it back. I can't trust him not to hurt me. So instead of talking anymore, I get on my tiptoes and kiss him.

FIFTEEN

STAY

"I might have to call the PDA police." Simone glides up to my locker just as Joel's leaving. "Later, Ryder," she says. He waves and disappears. I touch my mouth, still warm from his lips. Simone looks at me and rolls her eyes.

"Come on," I say, switching books. "Be happy for me."

"Oh, don't get me wrong; I'm happy for you," she says. "I'm just making an observation."

"Which is?"

"That you two are zero to sixty—there's no slow lane. No on-ramp. I just don't want you to crash and burn."

"Nice car analogy," I scoff.

"I thought so," she says with a hair toss.

"Maybe you should place a bet," I joke, but it comes out a little biting. At first, people gossiped about the kiss at the party. Then they whispered about me being the wrecking ball that brought down the house of Joel and Lauren. And finally, they started placing wagers on how long we'd last.

"Never," Simone says quietly. "Hey." She waits until I look at her. "You have everything you wanted," she says. "I mean, if Joel's constant hallway kisses are any indication, he doesn't care who knows how he feels about you." She pauses. "All I want is for you to be happy. I just wonder about the speed of this thing. Like, maybe, take it a little slower?"

I shut my locker and start toward class. "We're fine," I tell her. "It's going to be fine."

Probably sensing my annoyance at her admittedly legitimate concern, Simone complains—*again*—about being grounded for Friday's missed curfew, then changes the subject to Felicity's newest fashion accessory: a Slinky. As a bracelet. As she rambles on, I get lost in my head, thinking about Joel. About his kisses. About the satisfaction of knowing that I'm his girlfriend, even if it comes packaged with a seemingly permanent position in the gossip-filtered spotlight. But mostly, about how I *did* get everything I wanted.

As I turn into our math classroom, I have to shove off that thought's footnote:

If I got everything I wanted, then why am I left wanting more?

The week before the Electric Freakshow concert, I start to wonder if Joel's been switched with an alien doppelgänger because he's so . . . *happy*. Happy like I've never seen him. Happy like maybe he's never been in his life. Across the room in English, he gives me actual, full-fledged smiles, as opposed to the half smiles that looked almost painful for him to bring to the surface before. There's more fire in him—more bounce in his step. At one point, I consider asking him if he started taking uppers.

"Groupie looks good on you," I say with a laugh as we stroll through the parking lot at lunch on Thursday. "I don't think I've ever seen you this pumped."

"Really?" he asks, raising his eyebrows like he's shocked by the observation. I can't help but wonder who Joel sees in the mirror every day.

"Seriously," I say. "You're normally more . . . sedate."

He laughs out loud, and it makes me feel like the sun is shining on my insides. We're next to his car, and he walks with me to the passenger side, then leans against me so I'm resting on the door. The metal is cold, but his body is like a blanket. He looks at me seriously.

"I'm excited to go to the show for sure," he says, his dark eyes burrowing into me. "They're amazing live. But mostly? I'm excited to go with you."

My breath catches a little—this *is* Joel we're talking about.

"I'm excited to go with you, too," I say earnestly. He bends down and grazes my lips with his own, then steps away and moves around the car to the driver's side.

"Come over after school?" he asks, unlocking the car. We both get in and I shiver in my seat. "I've got some old live shows to play for you." I nod automatically; hanging out after school has become our thing.

"Sounds great," I say, glancing down at my phone. A text from Simone just came through—a text with a lot of sad face emoticons in it.

"Okay if I call Simone?" I ask Joel. "She's really bummed about this whole being grounded thing. I think she needs me to talk her off the ledge. I mean she's talking about joining a *club* just so she won't have to go straight home from school— it's a serious situation. But I'll try not to be too long."

Joel puts the car in reverse and gives me one of those unpredictable smiles; my arms get goose bumps. "I get it; no worries," he says. "Take your time, Linus."

As he turns to look behind us while he backs the car out of the space, I can't deny that I cringe a little. My nickname's not right coming from him. Then again, I think as he shifts to drive and navigates us out of the lot, at least he feels comfortable enough with me to call me by a nickname in the first place. So there's that.

After school, I step from the biting cold into the enveloping warmth of Joel's house, and he immediately wraps his arms around me in the entryway.

"I made you hot chocolate," he says into my hair.

"You did not," I say, pulling back, surprised. He nods, then kisses me—a lingering peck. I'm not afraid that anyone will see us: I know his mom is working.

"That's really sweet," I say, thinking that it really is. And also wondering if he made hot chocolate for Lauren.

"I took the mugs up to my room," he says, "and I've got the first DVD cued up. I can't wait to play it for you. I figured we could watch one each day so we're primed for next week."

I laugh as he takes my hand. We walk upstairs and both settle onto floor pillows. Joel presses play on the DVD and I take a sip from the mug in front of me—I have to say that he did a pretty decent job. We listen to the first song in silence: It's one of EF's early radio hits, "Shooting Stars," and seeing them play it onstage is a whole different experience. I can't wait to see them for real.

I shift on my pillow, thinking that it's lumpy. Then I remember thinking the same thing yesterday and the day before—I realize that I've sat in the same spot every time I've been here. Is this *my* pillow? Do we have his and her pillows already? I wonder whether we're on relationship autopilot—until the song switches and Joel switches things up too. He pulls me to my feet.

"Dance with me," he says. The song is one of the slowest, most sentimental songs in the Freakshow arsenal. It's called "Flannel." "Did you know he wrote this for his childhood sweetheart?" Joel asks as he pulls me close. We sway to the music, draped around each other like fabric ourselves.

"Really?" I murmur into his broad shoulder. "That's so sweet."

"She broke his heart eventually," he says. Then, after a beat, "I feel like I might suffer the same fate with you."

I pull back, eyes wide. "Why would you say that?"

"I don't know; I just feel like . . . maybe I'm the heavy."

"The heavy?" I ask, glancing at him again but then resting my cheek on his chest. "What are you talking about?"

"Haven't you ever heard that?" he asks. "In a relationship, there's always someone who likes the other person more. They are heavier . . . because they're carrying stronger feelings around all the time. I'm the heavy."

"I think a heavy is actually someone who's protection for someone else—like a bouncer or something."

"Whatever, it's what I call it," he says. "It's what Lauren and I used to call it."

The mention of Lauren makes me take a step back; my arms fall to my sides. I'm still not completely comfortable with Joel's explanation of why she was at his house on Halloween, and I don't want even the idea of her here now. I'm jealous; I'm jealous of her ghost in our relationship.

"I didn't mean to bring her up," Joel says, sensing my hostility.

"It's okay," I say, stepping toward him again. *I can be better than Lauren,* I think. Joel hates jealousy, so I won't show him my feelings.

"What I was trying to say was that I feel like I like you more than you like me," Joel says, looking into my eyes, strong and steady. "And that worries me a little, because I think I'm falling in love with you."

I've never heard those words from a boyfriend before, and the jolt of them is like lighting. I want to say it back, but I kiss him instead. Hard. So hard that he hesitates for the tiniest moment—maybe for being caught off guard—before he matches my intensity. I don't realize how close we are to the open door to Joel's room until he reaches out with his leg and kicks it shut. *Slam!* The song changes to a faster, pounding beat—"Magnets for Fate"—and it fuels my fire.

Joel grabs the hem of my sweater and pulls it up over my head; I let him do it because there's a tank top underneath and I've lost a layer or two with him before. But then he pulls me down onto the bed: not our usual make-out spot.

Joel kisses me on my mouth, my neck, and the top of my chest where skin's visible above my tank top. I close my eyes and lose myself in the moment and the music. He pushes up the bottom of my shirt so my stomach's showing; with his warm palm on my ribs, he kisses to the right of my belly button, then his mouth is on my jaw and my ear and my lips again. We kiss more recklessly than usual, and when I feel his fingers working the top button of my jeans, I don't think about it at all.

There's a girl somewhere inside me, telling me that I don't really want to do this right now. But there's duct tape over her lips. I'm not listening, because I feel young and powerful and possessed by the song and the kisses and somehow I don't care that I can't hear what she's saying.

Lots of people have done it, I think when Joel pauses and raises his eyebrows in question just before it happens. *He and Lauren have done it.* I'm not sure who I am when I nod. *Yes.*

But then, when he's lying flat on top of me, when his face is smashed into the pillow, when he's breathing hard and whispering how much he loves me, he really does, tears slide down my cheeks into my hair. I wipe them away before he sees, knowing it would make him feel bad.

Would it?

When he goes to get water from downstairs, I fake a call from home and claim to be in trouble for missing dinner. He doesn't even question it, even though it's barely five o'clock.

Then I practically run out the front door, regret already creeping through my veins. I know it; I know it before I even get home. I let Joel take too much—and as I think about it, I don't even know why. I'm not in love with Joel Ryder. In this moment, I'm not even sure I know the real him at all.

Back in my own room, the one with my own playlist, the duct tape's off and the girl in my head is screaming *No!* at me. I want to scream too, but I'm too busy crying instead. I pace in front of my dresser, wishing I had a time machine. I want a jump-back button on my life. I want to blast myself back twenty minutes and say "stop." I want to gather up my things and go, sure of myself and who I am. I want my virginity back. I want my *me* back.

I pause and turn to my reflection in the mirror above my dresser. My face is red and blotchy, and there's a mark low on my neck from where Joel was kissing me. But when I get to my eyes, I don't recognize the girl I see in the mirror.

I can't look at her anymore, so I turn out the light.

FIFTEEN

GO

I haven't spoken to my brother since seeing him on campus, and as I walk through the halls at school, I'm convinced I've been transported to bizarro-land. People are staring at me, covering their mouths to whisper as I pass. "You've got to be kidding," I murmur, trying to pretend not to notice. I have to try pretty damn hard.

I slide into my seat for homeroom and stare at a blank notebook page. That's when I can hear the conversations around me. Aaron and Tricia broke up in dramatic fashion over the weekend.

Aaron stays silent behind me, but Tricia is noticeably absent. I wonder how bad their split was.

"I heard it was because of the new girl."

My breath catches, but I try not to react to the comment. I'm pretty sure I'm not the new girl they could be talking about; there's no way I'm involved in this. Whether it was him or his friends who liked me, I told Aaron that I had a boyfriend. The girl behind me whispers something that I can't hear, and then there's a giggle.

Freaking hell.

I gnaw on my thumbnail as my heart pounds. Mr. Powell finally takes attendance and then squeaks his marker across the board. It's like a hundred sets of eyes are watching me—and all I want is for the fire alarm to go off so I can make a grand escape.

I turn to look out the window as some of the last of the orange and yellow leaves fall from the trees to the frosty school lawn. I remember when the colors first started changing in September. Gram and I went for a drive in the country, something she said she'd never get tired of doing. We stopped to buy a half gallon of cider from a vendor on the side of the road and then went home to start a fire—even though it wasn't cold. Gram said it was all about the atmosphere. Gram was the atmosphere.

The trickle of a tear running down my cheek startles me, and I sniffle hard and wipe it away. It seems like all of my happy memories with her have been drowned out by my guilty ones, but this is nice. It's nice to remember how beautiful my life once was.

"Miss Cabot? Is there a problem?" Mr. Powell calls.

"What?" I ask, glancing over. The room is watching me, pencils poised as if they've been taking notes while I was staring out the window, daydreaming. "Sorry," I say. I reach quickly to grab a pen from my backpack as whispers start again behind me.

"Told you," the same voice who blamed me for the breakup says. I shoot a look at the girl, and she makes a face as if disgusted that I would dare acknowledge that she's gossiping about me. Without meaning to, my eyes find Aaron's and he mouths, "Sorry," like I should know what he's talking about.

I spin back around, my cheeks burning from a shame I don't even deserve, and count down the minutes to lunch. What could that idiot have possibly said to make the entire school think I was involved in his breakup? Who are these people?

I start copying down the new bell schedule from the board and hope that Tricia doesn't come wandering in. Because right now her being absent seems to be the only thing keeping this day from getting completely out of control.

To which the universe answers by letting her walk in the door.

After class ends, I'm halfway down the hall when someone grabs my elbow. I turn, afraid that I'm about to be harassed right here in front of everyone.

"Sorry," Aaron says, his smile broadening when I meet his eyes. I yank my arm from his grip, glancing around cautiously as the stares of other students zero in on us. "I just wanted to talk to you for second."

"So not a good idea," I say, and start to walk off.

"Caroline," he calls quickly. "The rumors . . . they're not my fault. I don't want you to think—"

"No offense, Aaron," I say, lowering my voice as I move back toward him. "But I don't even know you. And I'm not really looking to. So can we just agree to stay away from each other or something?" Okay, that might have sounded a bit harsh. He winces as if to prove the point.

"Trish and I broke up," he says. "And I know it's not right to—"

I groan. He's just not getting it. I'm not interested in Aaron, and it has nothing to do with whether or not he has a girlfriend. With another explanation seeming pointless, I slip away, keeping my head down to block out the prying eyes, the whispers.

I walk straight to the girls' bathroom, where I can escape for at least a few minutes. It's like there's a pressure building, and I don't know how to stop it. I go to stand at the white porcelain sink and check my reflection. I stare, willing myself not to look away. But even now, even after all this time, I still can't meet my own eyes. I'm starting to wonder if I ever will.

"Well, don't you look just lost?"

I spin around and see Tricia standing in the doorway, her hair pulled back into a high bun. Next to her is another girl— short and stocky and wearing a pair of tan work boots. My heart nearly leaps from my chest.

"Look, I—"

Tricia holds up her hand as if telling me to save it, then she starts in my direction, stopping at the sink next to me as if she's just in here to wash her hands. Her friend continues to eye me from the doorway. I get the sick sense that she's blocking it. I let my backpack fall to my feet and turn to Tricia.

"I didn't steal your boyfriend," I say, trying to sound braver than I feel. "So if that's what everyone's saying, it's not true."

Tricia arches an eyebrow at her reflection as she pumps some soap into her palm. She runs her hands under the water as if she isn't intimidating me practically into tears.

"Aaron said you were cute," she says. "Actually, the word he used was *adorable*." She looks sideways at me. "You are, aren't you?"

I have no idea what she wants me to say, but I'm starting to get pissed. "Look, I'm sorry that he said that—the feeling isn't mutual. But I don't want to be involved in your—"

"Caroline," she says abruptly. "That's your name, right? Well, it's too late for your lies. Aaron and I are over, and I think we both know why."

I widen my eyes. "No. I don't actually."

She scoffs. "Do you think I'm stupid? Do you think I haven't seen the two of you talking? I haven't liked you from the first second you walked through those doors, *Caroline*." She leans toward me, lowering her voice. "And I don't need a reason to hate you. I just do. So maybe you should run back to whatever hick town you came from."

I scowl, offended that she's trash talking my town. Angry that she thinks it's okay to just hate and threaten me for no reason. Who does that? I put my hand on my hip and stare her down. "Has anyone ever told you that you're a complete bitch?" I ask.

I don't have time to react before Tricia's wet hand is knotted in my hair, her fist trying to find my face. I scream, grabbing for her hair, but the bun prevents me from getting any leverage. We crash back into the tiled wall, and it knocks the air out of my lungs. In that moment of vulnerability, Tricia's knuckles connect with my cheek—sending me sideways toward the toilets.

I try to fight back, even have the consciousness to attempt some of the shots that Chris taught me. But when I feel a heavy boot kick the back of my knee, I go down. And then all that's left to do is curl up and cover my head.

I try not to cry. I'm sitting in a blue-upholstered chair in the principal's office, looking on as she fills out a form before sliding it in a manila folder with my name on it. My body hitches each time I take a breath, tears ready to spill over at any second. I'm embarrassed that I got jumped. I'm sorry that I didn't get in even one decent punch. And I'm mad as hell that someone would do this for no good reason. I hate school. I hate *this* school.

"Miss Cabot," the principal says, her eyes suspicious behind her glasses. "I don't understand. The other girls say that you started this. You called Miss Allen a bitch."

I point to my face, the spot where my cheek is throbbing— the skin raised and turning black and blue. "Last I checked," I say, "I'm the only one with bruises. Did it occur to you that they cornered me in the bathroom?"

"Yes, it occurred to me," she says, seeming moved by my shaky voice. She reaches to pluck out a tissue and then hands it to me over the desk. When I take it, she presses her lips together in a show of sympathy. "Regardless of how it started, it's district policy to suspend all parties involved."

"What?" I snap. "I didn't *do* anything!"

"I'm sorry, Caroline. The other girls have already been escorted off campus, and they'll be out until next Monday. The length of time is at my discretion, so how about you return on Thursday?"

"Are you asking or telling me?" I say, ready to run out and never come back. I can't believe this is my life.

The principal exhales. "Telling."

I nod, grabbing my backpack from the floor and wincing at the weight. There's probably a boot-size bruise on my shoulder and another on my thigh, but I refuse to let it stop me from escaping this madhouse. I walk through the empty halls on my way out the front door and into the rain. And the minute I'm inside my car, I cover my face and cry.

I don't text Chris or Simone about the fight. I'm not sure why—I guess I'm ashamed, even though I shouldn't be. Instead I drive back to my *hick town*, looking for something. Comfort that I know is no longer there.

I pull to the curb in front of Gram's house, bumping it with my tire. I whimper when I see the SOLD sign on her front lawn, struck with the thought that it's all over now. She's really gone. I miss her so much—I'm not sure how I'll ever survive it.

"I need you," I say, looking up at the ceiling of my car. "I can't do this without you." I wait there a long time, wishing away the pain in my face, the pain in my heart. "I didn't tell you enough," I say quietly, letting the tears streak down my bruised cheeks, "but I love you, Gram. I love you more than anyone. And if I could do it all over again, I would have stayed."

I plan to sit there all afternoon, but after only a few minutes my phone buzzes and startles me. I see my dad's cell phone number on the caller ID.

"Hi." My voice is thick with tears, my lips raw from crying.

"Caroline," he says. "My God, where are you? The school called and said you got in a fight. Are you okay?"

I'm quiet. I don't want to alarm him or ask for sympathy. I have no desire to talk about the fight or relive what it was like to be helpless on the floor while two people kick your ass. So when he says my name again, I answer as simply as I can. "No. I'm not okay."

SIXTEEN

STAY

There's no way I'm getting out of bed.

Rain pounds against my window like the sky is crying with me. I go over it again and again, the ten minutes . . . no, *two* minutes that changed me forever. Regret tries to eat me alive. *He said he loves me,* I think. *Does that make it all right?* I laugh bitterly at myself, thinking of all the times I said casually to Simone, "I love Joel." Beautiful Joel. But it was a crush. It wasn't love. And his words yesterday—they were just words, too. I didn't *feel* them. I should have never—

My phone buzzes.

YOU WERE EPIC.

My stomach lurches and I roll to my side, curling my legs up to my chest. I am so disappointed by him. I want him to instinctively know how badly I need to talk about what happened instead of just calling it *epic* and moving on to FREAK-SHOW IN ONE WEEK! STOKED?

I type back SURE and wonder if he'll get it. If he'll hear me.

Ask me what's wrong. Ask me how I'm feeling. Ask me anything about me so I will know that you care, so I'll know that I'm wrong to feel like I gave myself to someone . . . unworthy.

Instead what buzzes through is GOTTA GO. SEE YOU IN CLASS.

The simple words sit heavy on my chest, and I lie still, almost like I'm not breathing at all, until Mom comes in a few minutes later, telling me I'm going to be late for school. I can't help but wonder whether I look different to her. Because I *feel* different. And definitely not in a good way.

When I walk into school, the halls are nearly empty—I'm late. Almost to my locker, I smell lavender from somewhere. It's faint and then it's gone, but it reminds me of Gram.

It's been over a month since she died, and I'm starting to forget things about her. I can't picture her face as well. Hear her voice as well. If I could, I think, looking for any excuse, maybe I'd know how to make better choices.

I swap out the books from home for my English binder, but when I consider sitting through class with Joel, my chest feels like it's caving in. So, snap decision made, I toss the binder back in my locker and go to the library to hide in the stacks. The librarian will give me a pass—I'll tell her I'm researching a paper. It'll be fine.

I spend the morning ignoring Joel or writing back one word answers to his texts. When ONE MORE DANCE? comes through, thankfully I'm already in Simone's car or I might run to the auditorium and punch him.

"Ugh." I sigh aloud.

"What?" Simone asks. I haven't told her about last night. Despite being positive that she'll be supportive, I'm too ashamed. So, I have a secret—but I'm not keeping it to hold it close. I'm keeping it to bury it.

"Just my mom," I lie. Thankfully, her favorite pop princess comes on the radio to distract her from asking more.

I eat nothing at the diner: Food is disgusting. And after lunch, when Simone and I part in the hallway, supposedly headed for class, I turn toward the main doors instead.

For the first time in my life, without even giving it much thought, I ditch school.

Later I'm lying in bed, staring at the white sky outside my window, when my mother comes in. "Caroline," she says, her brow furrowed. I have a quick worry that she found out about my skipping school, but then she keeps talking. "Teddy just called," she says. "He asked if you'd come to dinner at your father's tonight."

I haven't seen my father since Halloween, even though I promised to come back soon. I can't even remember the last time I saw my brother. Hell, even Natalie is a shadow. It occurs to me that I'm avoiding everyone.

"I don't feel like it," I say. It strikes me that I don't *feel* like anything. I'm a shell of a person.

"Are you sick?" my mom asks, looking concerned.

"No," I say. "I just don't want to drive all the way to Clinton." *I don't want to move.*

"I understand," Mom says, "but it's good to go now so that you can spend Thanksgiving with us. Your aunt Claudia is coming back." She pauses. "It's our first holiday without Mom and, well, I'm going to need you by my side, Caroline."

My unfocused eyes find hers. Suddenly I'm so sick of hearing about how she needs me that leaving is the only option. Running is the answer.

"Fine," I say, lugging myself from the mattress. I walk over to my closet to yank a Clinton sweatshirt off the hanger. As I'm working my knotted hair back into a ponytail, my mother continues talking, saying how my sister is going to be on the dean's list this year. I walk past her and out into the hall. I don't even say good-bye before leaving.

I drive to Clinton, and when I stop in front of my father's house, I think of driving away. Of ditching dinner, too. But then I notice my stepmother peeking out of the living room window. I've been spotted.

I start toward the two-story house, walking like the life has been sucked out of me. *Who knows? Maybe it has.* I ring the bell and blow out my breath just before the front door opens.

"Hey, sweetheart," my father says warmly. But unlike last time, his words seem more hollow. I want to ask him where he's been the last five years, how he let this happen to me. But I just force a smile and let Dad lead me into the kitchen, where Debra is making some sort of saucy meat concoction. My dad tells me that Teddy's not coming because he has a test tomorrow and needs to study. The minute my father turns his back, I text my brother: YOU LEFT ME!

I genuinely smile when Teddy writes back, PULL ON YOUR BIG-GIRL PANTS. YOU'RE FINE.

Dad and I end up in the living room where he quickly leaves to get me something to drink. I stare at the muted TV, the photos on the wall. There's one of Gram in the dining room; I can't look at it right now. When Dad's back, we sit in awkward silence for a few seconds before he decides to take control of the conversation.

"How's school?" he asks.

I shrug. "Fine." *Sip.*

"Grades are good?" he asks.

I nod. "Yep."

"Simone?"

"She's fine." I sip again, trying to think of something else to say. Then, "The same as always: loud and funny. She always has my back." *I didn't tell her about Joel,* I think. *I'll never tell her.*

"Everyone needs a Simone in their life," Dad says, finishing his own drink and setting it aside. "I know your gram's death has been hard on you, Coco. If there's anything—"

"Dinner's ready!" Debra calls from the other room. I've never been so thankful for an out from a conversation as I am in this moment. I mumble a thanks to my father, and then we move into the dining room, which looks like it was decorated out of a fancy catalog—I'm a little afraid to touch anything. The table is set for three, but there seems to be enough food for three hundred.

"I guess I went a little overboard," Debra says, looking embarrassed. I can see how much she wants me to like her. If I were in a different head space, I might. But right now, she's just trying too hard.

"I love leftovers," Dad says when I don't answer. He goes over and kisses her on the forehead with adoration so pure that it stings. Way back before the divorce, he used to kiss Mom's forehead, but never like that.

Dinner consists of small talk between the adults and short responses from me when prompted. The food is actually good—Debra is a better cook than Mom, which may be why Dad has a bit of a belly now.

At the end of the night, Dad and Debra offer up their newly redecorated guest room, but I just thank them and smile my fake smile. I text Mom that I'm leaving because she made me promise that I would, then take the long way through the middle of campus to get back to the highway. The old brick buildings are spotlit from the ground up so that kids can find their way.

I stop at a four-way sign, and a group of scarf-wearing, coffee-at-night-carrying students crosses the street. It's two guys and three girls, and one of the guys says something so funny that all three of the girls toss back their heads like horses when they laugh at him. The guy's cute—he's blond and all-American-looking but not in an over-the-top way. He's in a plaid shirt with a puffer vest and his cheeks are flushed from the cold. It seems like any one of the girls could be his girlfriend, and when the tall dark-haired one takes his arm, I guess it's her.

I'm staring at him when halfway across the street, out of nowhere, he looks at me. Our eyes hold each other's long enough for the girl to slap him playfully on his chest. I feel a pang of loss when he turns away.

I watch the group disappear, feeling something like familiarity for Mr. Hilarious. I wonder if he's a friend of Teddy's and think back to when I met a bunch of them at his dorm. I'm lost in thought when the car behind me beeps. I drive through the intersection, craning my neck for one last glimpse at the guy. But he's gone.

SIXTEEN

GO

My father takes Tuesday off from work and stays home with me, occasionally looking at my cheek underneath the ice pack he bought just for this occasion. He's sweet—never once asking what happened, or even funny, like when he calls me Rocky Balboa. All in all, his simple presence makes it better.

I tell Chris that I'll be at my mother's for a few days to help her sort through my gram's belongings (which has already been done) so that he won't come by and find me battered and bruised. All I want right now is to erase the last month of my life—erase every day since my gram had her stroke.

The week is quiet as I heal, and it isn't until Thursday morning at breakfast that my stepmother finally sets down her fork and stares at me. "Since your father is never going to ask," she says, shooting him a pointed look, "I will. What happened? Why on earth would anyone hit you like that? I saw the bruises when you walked down the hall from the shower. You have a footprint on your back, Caroline. I think we should press charges."

"It was a boot," I say, putting a soggy piece of waffle in my mouth. It's too sweet from syrup, too salty from butter. I nearly gag on it and then choke down an orange juice chaser. "I don't want to press charges," I say.

My father shifts in his seat, and I look up. His face is weary and distraught as he folds his hands in front of him on the edge of the table. "Do you want to move back to your mother's? I understand if—"

As he continues to talk, saying he'll support whatever decision I make, I think of Gram. What she would say if she were here. I twist the charm of her necklace with my fingers, and then all at once, like a dream, she's here. I don't see her or anything crazy like that. But I feel her—a sudden force that is equal parts hug and shove. She'd want me to be strong. She'd want me to stop running. To finally stop running.

"I'm not going to move," I tell my dad then, looking up at him. "I want to stay here with you and Debbie." My stepmother lets out a breath, as if she's been holding it in the entire time.

"Then we're happy to have you," my father says, smiling in a way that is so much like Teddy, I feel an actual pain at how much I miss my brother. Even if he's the one who owes me an apology for flipping out on me and my boyfriend.

. . .

I decide to let my dad call me in sick to school on Thursday and Friday. It doesn't take much convincing, especially since the bruise on my face is still really swollen. I have plans to meet up with Chris after the ritual Sunday dinner at my dad's, but when my brother calls around noon to say he isn't coming, I know I have to fix things with him. I send Chris a text: RAIN CHECK ON TONIGHT. SORRY. FAMILY STUFF.

I expect him to make a joke or say he's going to hunt me down anyway, but instead he writes back, MY FAULT?

I furrow my brow. NOT THIS TIME . . .

I'll have to tell Chris about the fight eventually, especially since he's going to see the bruises sooner or later. But first I'm going to meet up with Teddy and put the entire mess behind us.

It's after three when I finally get up the nerve to leave my house, the bruise on my cheek still noticeable even with a ton of Debbie's foundation. My brother doesn't know I'm coming, but I'm surprising him with his favorite—Debbie's homemade quiche—so he can't exactly turn me away.

Then again, I probably should have called, because nobody answers my brother's door as I pound on it. I realized when I got to his floor that I left my phone in the car—which is a clear indication that I must have a concussion.

I groan, thinking that Teddy and Phil are probably at the

library. I leave the covered pie plate on the floor next to their room. I'm halfway across the downstairs lobby when I realize that I didn't leave a note on the dry-erase board on his door. I should at least let my brother know that I'm the one who left the food.

I press the button for the elevator, but when the doors slide open, the world seems to drop out from under me. From inside the cramped space, Chris's eyes widen when he sees me standing there. His arm is slung carelessly over the shoulders of a pretty brunette while she's still mid-laugh. Quickly Chris pulls away. The girl offers me little more than a curious glance, but I know at once that she's Maria. Devastated, I take a step back.

Chris looks between me and Maria before opening his mouth. "Oh. No, I—"

"Shut up," I say, thinking back on everything Teddy said that day. Chris and I were supposed to be together tonight, but when I cancel, he comes here? He sees her? Has he been with her all week? A dagger, sharp and poisoned, twists in my gut.

I've been so stupid. I should have just stayed away, stayed in my old life with my family—my mother, sister, and Simone. Ever since Gram died, I've been reckless—running away from my problems, trusting people I shouldn't, getting jumped in the school bathroom. And it seems like everything horrible started right here. Right with Christopher.

I turn to leave. Chris jumps forward, grabbing my upper arm to spin me to him, but when he sees me up close, he gasps.

"Caroline, what happened to your face?" He puts his palm on my cheek as his eyes go panicked and feral. "Who did this to you?"

But my pride and heart are aching too much for me to tell him. I hate him for sounding so concerned, so protective. He's made a fool out of me, just like Teddy thought he would.

"Get off," I say, pushing him away. Behind him, Maria purses her lips and looks at the ground. I back toward the door, shaking my head. "Don't call me, Chris," I say. "Don't show up. Don't *anything*. I'm done."

I turn before he can touch me again, jogging toward the exit. I hear him cut after me, but I dodge to the right the minute I'm out of the building and then flatten myself against the outer wall while he runs toward the parking lot, screaming my name. The pain in his voice nearly unravels me, but I won't be just another girl to him. I wanted to be *the* girl.

It was only a coincidence that I parked on the street when I got to the dorm, but I'm glad as I make my way toward my car. My body is shivering, but it's not from the cold. This is what it's like to be hollowed out, to have hit rock bottom.

When I get in my car, I find my phone dropped down between two seats. I fish it out and stare down at the screen, not sure who to turn to anymore. Suddenly I think about

Debbie's words about needing family—about maybe needing a sister. I dial my mother's house, but when Natalie answers, I nearly hang up. I force myself to talk and ask in a cracked voice for our mother.

"Caroline," my sister says. "What's happening? You sound weird."

I close my eyes and listen to the hum of my engine as I let my car heat up. I'm not sure where to start—so I go back to the beginning. "I'm sorry I wasn't there when Gram died," I whisper. "I hate myself for it, Natalie. I would do anything to take it back."

My sister takes in a harsh breath, speechless for a moment. "I shouldn't have said those things to you," she says. "You had every right to go out that night, Coco. You didn't do anything wrong."

The affection in her voice makes me feel like we're kids again, sneaking to look at our Christmas presents under the tree while our parents were still asleep. Natalie and I weren't always this far apart. We used to be friends.

"I'm having a really bad week," I choke out finally, adjusting the rearview mirror to look at my face—actually *look* at my face. I'm shocked by what I see, the distortion in skin tone, the swelling. The utter sadness in my eyes.

"Nat?" I ask. "Are you busy right now? I could use someone to talk to."

"You're willing to talk to me again?" she asks, a little teasingly. "Of course, Caroline. Are you at Dad's?"

"I'm on my way home now."

"Then I'll meet you there," she says. "And hey, I'll even bring the bottle of wine Aunt Claudia left behind."

I choke out a laugh. "Don't you think she'll ask about it when she comes in for Thanksgiving?"

"Naw," Natalie says. "She'll just bring more. I'm going to throw on sweats and head over. I'll see you soon."

I let out a held breath as I hang up. Even though it's been years since my sister and I have been close, it seems almost too easy. In a way, I think maybe I never really lost her at all. And so with the comfort of that thought, I leave the Clinton campus, letting the hurt fade rather than trying to bury it.

SEVENTEEN

STAY

I'm swimming in a tank, watching the humans go by. I'm underwater, so I can't hear them. I'm a fish, so I don't speak their language. Mostly I don't know the word "happiness"—it doesn't seem to apply to me anymore—but I'm not sad either. I'm just here—sitting on Joel's beanbag chair playing the role of girlfriend in the fake movie version of my life. Watching the formerly mellow male lead bounce off the walls about Friday's Electric Freakshow concert.

"I'm so glad your mom didn't find out that you skipped class again. I still can't believe you did that. And here I thought you were such a good girl." He grins, something mischievous, flirtatious. But it only turns my stomach.

"She's kind of clueless most of the time," I say flatly. The thought of getting in trouble doesn't deter me. In fact, I'm thinking of cutting history tomorrow.

Joel's moved on. "I looked up the set lists online. I think they might open with 'Magnets for Fate.' I hope they do: That would be so badass."

You used to be so reserved—I guess this is what amps you up. Or have you been brainwashed?

Have I?

"My mom's letting me take the Suburban," he says from across the room. "We can take a few more people if Simone and her man-of-the-week want to ride with us."

"Don't talk about her like that," I snap. Joel tosses a pillow at me.

"You know I'm joking," he says. "Simone's cool."

"Yes." I look at him sternly. "She is." I watch him walk into his closet to flip through his assortment of hoodies. "Besides," I say. "Simone's not coming."

"Why not?" he calls, not looking back. "How could she miss it? I mean, they probably won't get back to the city for another two ye—"

"I already told you a million times," I say, annoyed. "She's *grounded*." I suddenly realize that Simone's a sweet talker—that she's gotten passes from her parents before while grounded. That maybe it's something more. I haven't told Simone that I slept with Joel, but I'm not exactly great at hiding things either. She knows I'm lying to her about something, and she thinks I'm madly in love with Joel Ryder and have ditched her every night for him. But in reality, I've been spending it in my room. Alone. Simone can't make me forgive myself, and she can't bring Gram back. Those are the only two things I want—and they're impossible.

"What's Simone doing with her tickets?" Joel asks. "Does she want us to scalp them? Because if so, we have to leave even earlier."

"We're already leaving at four," I say, rolling my eyes. "That's early enough."

"Baby," Joel says, turning toward me again. His eyes are bright, and he's smiling, but the word "baby" does nothing to endear me now. "I'd have gone last week if I could," Joel continues. "But, hey, at least we get to go together."

"At least," I mutter. I want to sprint away from this place, from this life. But the lead in my shoes is the fact that in a few days, I'll get to see my favorite band of all time. Music is the only thing that reaches me inside the fishbowl. So when Joel leans down to kiss me, I just close my eyes. And pretend I'm somewhere else.

Natalie has night class tonight, but I call her on the way home. I never told her about Gram's necklace, and although I know it's part of why I've been avoiding her, the thought of going alone with Joel to the concert has me almost panicked.

"Hey," I say when she picks up. "I was calling to see if

you're not too busy on Friday night, maybe you could come with me as I try to persuade River Devlin to marry you."

"I love him!" Natalie screams into the phone. "Wait . . . how do *you* know I love him?"

"I heard you on the phone," I say. "Anyway, Simone isn't using her two tickets, and if you want to go—"

The sound of Natalie's even louder screams on the other end of the line cut me off and make me hold the phone out from my ear. "So that's a yes, then?" I ask when she's finished.

"Yes!" she says excitedly. "Yes, definitely. Oh, wow, this is going to be awesome. I have to start planning what to wear."

"I'll help you pick something," I say. The voice coming out of my mouth sounds like someone else's, someone normal. "If you're going to snag a rocker, a sweater set won't cut it."

Natalie laughs, and later, after I hang up—I'm glad I called her.

SEVENTEEN

GO

"Tricia's back," the girl behind me says when I sit down in homeroom Tuesday morning. I turn tentatively, not sure if she's talking *to* me this time. When she nods, reaffirming that she is, I feel my heart sink. I might have been hoping Tricia would never return.

"Don't worry," the girl says. "If she touches you again, we've got your back." She motions to the blonde next to her.

"Yeah," her friend adds. "That was messed up. Two on one is some nasty stuff and totally not cool. Not to mention Aaron's a douche nozzle anyway."

I laugh, unable to stop myself from glancing over at Aaron. He's wearing his varsity jacket as he stares down at his folded hands, looking miserable. He was one of the first people to talk to me yesterday, saying that it was all a misunderstanding. I didn't stick around to listen to his pathetic ramblings, though. Looking at his sorry self now, I might even forgive him—if I didn't completely resent him for dragging me into his drama.

The door opens and Tricia pauses at the entrance, her normally slicked-back hair loose around her face. I'm surprised to see the embarrassment in her eyes, the way she looks at her shoes as she walks to her seat. The tough girl I remember from the bathroom is smaller now, even if only in presence.

"Heard her parents freaked," the girl behind me says. When I turn to her, she smiles. "I'm Darcy, by the way. Sorry I was a wench before. I'm not exactly a people person."

"She usually hates them," the other girl chimes in.

"Anyway," Darcy says as we wait for Mr. Powell to show up. "Tricia's suspended from the cheerleading squad for the rest of the season for"—she uses finger quotes—"'unbecoming behavior.'"

"What about the chick with the boots?" I ask, still able to feel their weight.

"Rita? Oh, she doesn't care about you. Probably doesn't even know your name." She turns to her friend. "She's cool now, right?"

The girl nods. "Yeah, she said she has no beef." They smile as if I should be happy, but I'm not. Not exactly.

"Thanks," I say, twisting in my seat. I check my phone, knowing that normally I could text Chris—let him cheer me up. But there are no missed messages. No calls. We really are over.

Almost immediately after I put my phone away, Darcy taps my shoulder with a note. I unfold it, checking the clock to see we still have another minute or two before class. I'm stunned to see it's from Tricia. Her pretty handwriting curls down the page in what can only be described as an apology letter without an actual apology.

She tells me that she's been forbidden from dating Aaron ever again, that she's been banned from cheerleading, and the best part—her parents made her write this letter. I try not to laugh, knowing it will seem cruel, even if it's out of disbelief. By the time I get to the end, I think about saving the paper to show Simone because there's no way she'll believe the nerve of this girl.

I decide to be the bigger person and hand Tricia back her humiliation. But first I scribble "TRUCE" at the top.

"Linus," Simone says as she turns to look up at me from the chair. "I want it to be a deep red, so put tons on."

I roll my eyes and squirt more dye into the pile of hair on top of her head that I've already saturated. We're in the bathroom at my father's house, spending a makeover night, a night without guys. "If I add any more dye," I tell her, massaging in the color, "you'll end up like Ronald McDonald."

"Sexy."

I finish and cover her scalp in a clear plastic shower cap. I hop on the sink counter as Simone sets the timer on her phone.

"So listen," she says. "We need to brainstorm who else to bring on Friday." She folds her hands in front of her. "So far it's just you, me, and Joel."

"What?" I ask with a laugh. Joel Ryder—now there's a name I haven't heard in a while.

"I offered it to him as a present to you," Simone says. "I got the tickets online the day they went on sale two months ago. I wanted to shove you two in the right direction. How was I supposed to know that you'd fall madly in love with someone else?" She stops and looks up at me apologetically. "Oh God, I'm sorry."

I shrug like it doesn't matter, pulling off the soiled gloves to drop them in the box of hair dye along with the used bottles.

"Still haven't heard from him?" Simone asks, her voice softer. When I told her what had happened, her first instinct was to find Chris and knee his privates. She settled on trying to find me a rebound instead. She said it was therapeutic.

"Nope. I guess he didn't love me all that much, huh?" Even though I try to sound resolved to the thought, it's killing me.

"He's an idiot," she says seriously, pain behind her own

eyes. I smile, glad that she's always here for me. Sorry that there was ever a time when I wasn't there for her. "Have you told Teddy about what happened?" she asks.

"No," I say. "I'm lying low. I haven't told anyone but you and Natalie."

Simone scrunches her nose. "Your sister Natalie? Where did this come from? Did she trade in her pitchfork and horns?"

"She's not so bad," I say. "She came over and hung out with me the day I saw Chris . . . ." I stop. "She's been great lately," I say instead. "Did you know she hasn't been on a date in nearly a year?"

"No wonder she's so bitchy all the time," Simone says before making kiss lips at herself in the mirror and checking her right, then left profile. "Maybe she needs to be set up or something." She widens her eyes at me. "Let's bring her to the concert! We'll give her an I'm-single-and-looking make-over and reintroduce her to the male species."

I crinkle my nose and start laughing. "Now I'm scared for her. Okay, so who else? Are any of Joel's other friends coming?"

"I'm not wasting a ticket on those losers," Simone says.

"Wait," I say to Simone. "How many tickets do you have?"

"Six—minus the one I gave Joel."

"How did you get so many . . . never mind," I say, shaking my head. "I probably don't want to know. But I might have someone to set my sister up with. It's almost creepy but at the same time—sort of awesome."

Simone's timer goes off on her phone. "Creepy doesn't sound promising," she says, sitting up straighter.

I hop down from the counter and lift the cap to check her color. "You're fully cooked," I say. After I give her a towel and start the water for her rinse, I smile. "I need a favor."

She groans and I spray her in the face *on accident*. "I need you to drop off those extra tickets at my brother's," I say. "I think he and Phil have a concert to get ready for."

Natalie and Phillip—how have I never had this stroke of genius before? They're both attractive, overachieving know-it-alls bent on making the people around them feel inferior. It's perfect, and honestly, I can't believe they've never seen it either.

Simone agrees to go to Teddy's, mostly because I think I'll have an anxiety attack if I step on the Clinton State campus so soon after dumping Chris. When she's gone, I go downstairs, but Dad and Debbie are out on a date night. The quiet, although peaceful at first, starts to close in around me. I call my sister.

Natalie sits next to me on the couch, passing the half-filled bottle of wine we still haven't finished in my direction. I take a sip, wince, and then tell her she can finish it. She laughs and sets it on the coffee table instead. When she rests back on the couch, Gram's initial necklace flashes at her throat. Turns out Gram had told her that she could have it. So when my sister saw me with the necklace, she burst into tears, thanking me for finding it. Considering how much I'd already lost and that I was finally on speaking terms with my sister, I let her keep it. If Gram wanted her to have it, then she deserves it.

"Natalie," I start in a quiet voice. "Do you think he's with her right now?" She doesn't ask who "he" is.

"Doubt it," she says. "If he ran after you like a madman, I'm guessing he feels pretty terrible."

"Good."

Natalie bumps her shoulder into mine and offers me the remote—the ultimate in pity. When I turn to her, I notice how much she resembles our mother. They have the same features, the same softness. For a second my sister fills the void I hadn't realized was there. I lay my head on her shoulder and stare blankly at the television.

"Have you ever loved anyone?" I ask. She swallows hard, then I feel her shake her head.

"No. I don't think I could ever let myself trust anyone enough to let them get that close. Maybe it was watching the brutal divorce, or maybe I was always this way. But believe it or not, Coco, I sometimes take myself a little too seriously."

I smile. "You don't say."

She's quiet but then turns to me. "Did you really love him?" she asks. "Not high-school-crush stuff—but bottom-of-your-heart, you-complete-me, rainbows-and-unicorns love?"

I laugh at the silliness of her definition, but after thinking it over—I decide that it's a fairly accurate description of how I felt about Chris. Still feel. "Yeah," I say, looking down. "That pretty much sums it up."

Natalie nods and then puts her arm around me, snatching the remote back from my hand. When she finds an old episode of *Project Runway* to watch, she sighs. "Then I really am sorry, Coco. I'm sorry he broke your heart."

I sniffle. "Yeah," I say. "Me too."

My phone vibrates in my pocket, and despite my vow to stop hoping, it wells up in my chest anyway. But the text that has popped up isn't the one I'm waiting for. It's my brother.

WHY DID SIMONE JUST GIVE ME AND PHIL CONCERT TICKETS?

I smile, knowing that Teddy and I will work out our problems eventually. He doesn't know about what happened with Chris, and I choose not to tell him now. Maybe I just want to bask in my denial for a little bit longer.

I hide the screen from my clueless sister next to me and write back, NATALIE + PHIL = AWESOME.

WHAT?!? I'M OPPOSED TO THIS IN SO MANY WAYS.

BUT IT SHOULD BE ENTERTAINING TO WATCH. LIKE TWO SHAKESPEAREAN MONKEYS AT THE ZOO.

I laugh and then text that I'll see him later. Natalie glances over just as I erase the message. "Who's that?" she asks.

"Simone. Oh, hey. So do you want to go to a concert this weekend? It's Electric Freakshow. . . ." My sister's cheeks start to redden and after a scream, giggle, and clap, she tells me that she loves Electric Freakshow (go figure). She starts to talk about what she'll wear, how her friends will trip out because the show has been sold out since tickets went on sale.

But as she talks, I sneak another look at my phone. I scroll though all my old messages, looking for one. And when I find it, the feeling is painful and at the same time soothing: I ONLY HAVE EYES FOR CAROLINE.

EIGHTEEN

STAY

There's a moment in Joel's mom's Suburban on the way to the Electric Freakshow concert when I have an out-of-body experience. I mean not really—I'm being dramatic. But as close to one as any sane person can get.

I see myself riding shotgun, Joel's hand resting a little too north of my knee. I should feel comfortable with it, but I don't. I swallow down bile that four antacids earlier couldn't fix. His other hand hangs over the steering wheel, James Dean style (without the cigarette), as we speed down the highway toward the city. In the middle seat behind me are Natalie and her friend Emma—gabbing away about recently posted tabloid photos of River Devlin and some supermodel—and Joel's friend Rod, who keeps sneaking glances at my sister's legs. Behind them are Joel's other friends Eric and Mike—they're chugging beer like it's water and they've just run a marathon.

I see all of us, heading to watch a band I've been obsessed with forever, out on a Friday night, young and alive. I see me with the guy I've pined for since before I was in a training bra and spending quality time with the sister I lost for so long. On paper, it's perfect.

But the thing about paper is: It burns.

Rod, Eric, and Mike force us to tailgate until the opening band starts its sound check; I sit on the open back of the truck people-watching, wishing I was with the strangers instead. All around me, laughter floats through the air. I feel like I might never genuinely laugh again.

"You seem out of it," Joel whispers into my ear. "Want to take a walk and talk?" He says "talk," but he licks the bottom of my earlobe. I want to shove him away, but I just sit there.

"I don't want to leave my sister," I say, looking over at her. She's sitting in a camp chair between Mike and Emma, laughing her face off. She feels my gaze and looks at me, beaming in a way I haven't seen from her since before our parents split.

"Hi, Coco!" she says loudly, waving.

"Hey, Nat," I say back, trying to make my voice sound . . . human.

"She looks all right to me," Joel whispers. He pulls back my hair and kisses my neck. "She'll be fine if we take off for a bit."

She might, but I won't.

"Get me a soda?" I ask in response. He pulls back and looks at me hard for a moment before shoving off the truck bed.

"At your service," he mutters under his breath as he walks away. "Wouldn't want to actually relax and have fun tonight or anything."

Finally we go inside and take our seats. Joel says he's going to buy us beer—that he thinks I need one. The comment makes me want to hit him. When he's gone, Natalie slides up next to me.

"Is everything okay?" she asks, genuinely concerned. "I mean, I know it's not—I can see it on your face. You've been gloomy the whole drive. What's happening?"

I love my sister for knowing, for caring about me even though I've been nothing but selfish toward her. I don't deserve her devotion.

"I lost Gram's necklace," I say, barely loud enough over the noise of the crowd. "I lied about not seeing it that day—I had it the entire time." I lower my eyes, unable to watch as her expression falters. "But then I lost it. I'm sorry I didn't tell you sooner."

Hate me, I think. But instead my sister grabs me and pulls me into a hug. "Thank you for telling me now," she says into my ear. "I hope this isn't the reason you've been avoiding me, Coco." She pulls back to look at me. "You're more important than a necklace."

A small smile tugs at my lips, relief breaking my chest in a tidal wave. I'm about to tell Natalie about my regrets with Joel, but then Emma comes running up and grabs Natalie's arm. Electric Freakshow is taking the stage.

I glance over toward the beer garden and Joel's not there; just before the lights go down, I see him, Rod, and Mike making their way toward the half wall that separates standing room from the seats. When a guard's not looking, they all hop it. Then it's black in the arena and he's gone. A few moments later, my phone buzzes. DOWN IN THE PIT—SO COOL! I'LL BE BACK UP FOR SECOND HALF.

NO WORRIES, I text back, relieved. ENJOY IT. I'VE GOT NAT TO KEEP ME COMPANY.

YOU'RE THE BEST GIRLFRIEND EVER, he writes back. I put my phone away without answering.

I know most of the playlist by heart, so I can't help but get lost in the music, and without Joel to remind me how much I hate myself, I even start having fun. Nat, Emma, Eric, and I sing at the top of our lungs and dance in the aisles as best we can in the sold-out stadium. I take off my jacket and pull back my hair. I'm parched and sweaty and for the first time in what feels like forever, I am alive.

But just when the night's done a one eighty, they play "Flannel," the song Joel and I were listening to in his room that day. Visions of his hands where I wish they'd never been crash into my brain.

"I need water!" I shout over the music to my sister. "I'll get you some too!"

She nods. "Want me to come with you?"

"No, I'm good!" I shout back. I squeeze by a half row of people and rush up the aisle to the concession stand, trying not to listen to the song that's rattling my bones. The opening song on the sound track to the biggest mistake of my life.

I step into the light and the music fades away; my ears still echo from drumbeats past. I move toward the nearest concession stand, but they're out of water, so I walk around the arena to the one on the other side. I get in line behind a blond guy wearing an inside-out red T-shirt—there are at least five people in line in front of him. I dig in my pockets to make sure I have money. The sound of fighting makes me look up.

"I saw the way you were looking at her," the woman in front of the blond guy says loudly to the man next to her. They're my parents' age; I guess Electric Freakshow appeals to a wide demographic.

"Who?" the man says, looking at her in disbelief. "Sasha, you've had too many of those blender margaritas. Let's get you a pretzel to soak up some of that crazy."

I hear the guy in front of me snort quietly just as I cover my mouth with my hand to stifle a giggle.

"Me crazy?" the woman says, her voice gaining in volume. "No, YOU crazy. I saw you looking at that fine young thing with the Madonna boobs and the Whitney hair."

Blond guy mutters "descriptive" under his breath, which makes me laugh out loud. I cover it up with a cough; the couple doesn't notice, but the guy turns around.

My eyes widen. "You," I say. "I've seen you before." He's cute, with bright blue eyes and messy hair that he tries to flatten now that I'm talking to him.

"Hopefully not on *America's Most Wanted*," he says. "It's been a few years, but they still run that one during hiatus. Or maybe it was my cameo on *All My Children*?"

"No, I think it was *Jeopardy!*" I say easily, smiling without thinking about it. "You lost because you didn't know who composed *Swan Lake*."

"Tchaikovsky," he says with a twinkle in his eyes. He points at himself. "Music major." Then he points at me. "Girl at the stop sign on campus last week?"

I nod, kind of thrilled that he remembers. And then suddenly I know where I've seen him before. "I also saw you at your friend's house after dropping off his hookup sweatshirt," I say.

"You hooked up?"

"No, my friend Simone."

"I know," he says. "My cover's blown. I've been stalking

your Facebook page for weeks. Hope that's not too weird." He pauses. "Yeah, of course it is. Sorry. My buddy Ed helped me track you down through your friend. I'm Chris, by the way. Your official stalker, I guess."

"It's nice to meet you, *Chris*," I say, taking a dramatic step back. He laughs, and when I look up to tell him I'm just joking and that it really is nice to meet him, the cashier interrupts our conversation.

"May I help you?" she calls impatiently like she's asked twice already. There's a huge space between Chris and the counter; all of the other patrons are done and gone except the fighting couple, now making out in the corner. Sick.

Chris blushes a little and says to me, "Hold that thought." He steps up, orders water and a pretzel, pays, and steps aside. I notice him lingering by the condiments, waiting for me as I pay for two waters.

"So?" Chris says when I approach. "You were saying?"

"First," I tell him, twisting the cap off my water to take a sip. "Why is your shirt on inside out?"

He chuckles, pulling out the fabric like he's surprised I'd ask. "Because it's an Electric Freakshow T-shirt."

"Uh . . ." I look around. "Then you're in the right place." I lean my hip against the condiment counter, taking another drink.

"Yeah, I know," he says, picking at the hem. "I just think

Electric Freakshow is overrated." He smiles at me. "Music major, remember?"

"Then why are you here, and more importantly, why are you wearing one of their shirts?"

He pauses then, his smile fading slightly. He darts a look in the direction of the seats but then shakes his head. "Misguided date." When I raise my eyebrows, he waves it off. "She already left," he adds. "But not before her boyfriend showed up and tossed his drink on me. I couldn't drive home smelling like beer, so my friend gave me a shirt. And although I appreciate the gesture, I have a moral responsibility to not advertise a mediocre band, so I turned it inside out."

I decide not to hold his Freakshow slams against him.

"What about you?" Chris asks. "Who are you here with?"

Joel.

At the thought of him, I take another hurried sip of water. Chris takes a bite of pretzel, and it's clear we're both kind of stalling. I smile at him. "You're such a music snob," I say.

"I really am. What about you? Are you—"

Someone grabs my elbow, and my heart leaps in my throat because I think Joel has found me.

"Coco?" Natalie says. I turn and see her standing there, sweaty and out of breath, with a surprisingly upset look on her face. She's holding a bundle of outerwear. Her jacket's on top, and it looks like it has blood on it.

"What's wrong?" I ask, looking around.

"Some guy elbowed Emma in the nose," she says. "He was dancing and flailing his arms around, and he accidentally hit her—she thinks it might be broken. She's in the bathroom, but she's bleeding everywhere. I think I need to take her to the hospital. Eric tried Joel's cell, but he's not picking up. I don't know what to d—"

"I've got a car here," Chris says, stepping forward. Natalie looks at him, surprised.

"Are you a friend of my sister's?" she asks.

He nods. "We go way back," he says, looking at me. "Right?"

"Totally," I say. "He'll take us. I'll go with you. I'll text Joel and tell him we left."

I'm aware of how excited I am to leave, despite the fact that I'm headed toward a night at the hospital instead of back to a concert with my . . . boyfriend. The word makes my stomach lurch, and I decide it's the last time I'll ever use it to describe Joel. But rather than tell him, I'm going to run off with Chris— I'm going to run away.

EIGHTEEN

GO

The show's already started when we finally get to the city—Simone apparently needed time to perfect her look. In carefully knotted braids, a too-tight EYE CANDY T-shirt, hot-pink arm warmers, and fuzzy boots, she's all sorts of adorable even when she's scowling at the full parking lots we pass. Finally we find a space; there's a collective exhale throughout the car—especially from Joel, who's been silently brooding in the backseat the entire way.

"You look great," Simone says to Natalie after we've all climbed out and are adjusting our clothes. Nat's in contacts and my denim skirt with tights, and I'll admit that she does look really pretty. "Now you, on the other hand," she says to me, motioning to my Electric Freakshow T-shirt and jeans, "*this* is not the fashionista I raised."

"Sorry," I say, grabbing a Clinton zip-up hoodie from the

front seat. "I didn't get the memo about the dress code." I look over at Joel and see him looking between our car and the venue, impatient like he's a forlorn groupie or something.

Simone and I lock eyes and then laugh. Joel Ryder—God, all the nights I wished to be doing what I'm doing now. And now everything's changed—we had nothing to talk about on the ride to the city. I wonder if we ever did.

We stash our valuables in the trunk and lock up. My sister is on the phone, telling Teddy to meet us at the south parking lot. I nearly lose it when she says, "Of course I think Phil's cool." She laughs like it's a stupid question. She's going to be so blindsided.

My brother and Phil are waiting on the curb at the end of the lot, Teddy texting someone on his phone while Phil looks more normal than I've ever seen him. I think he might even have used hair gel.

"Coco," Teddy calls as we cross the road toward them. I wave and we all rush over. "Chris isn't coming?" he asks.

I try not to wince at the mention of his name. "There's something I have to tell you," I say. "Although I need you to dial down your protective brother meter first."

He puts out his fingers and turns an imaginary knob, grinning at me like I'm crazy. "Done." In his other hand his phone lights up. "Hold on," he tells me.

Oh, sure. Let me just keep this secret in all night. I glance over to where Natalie and Phil are laughing about something, standing next to each other like old friends. It occurs to me that they are. That we all are. And that if Gram could see us now, she might even be a little proud that we showed up here together.

I lower my eyes, feeling the final break from my grief. Gram might even be a little proud of me.

"Sorry about that," Teddy says, putting his phone away before throwing his arm over my shoulders in an unexpected show of affection. "I've been trying to find a ticket all day," he says. "I thought I had a lead."

"Awesome," I say absentmindedly, looking over at Simone and Joel, talking to each other. She makes him laugh—actually laugh—and I wonder if maybe—

"Wait, who were you trying to get a ticket for?" I ask my brother, and he smiles like he's never smiled before.

"Doesn't matter," he says. "Now, why did I have to dial down my homicidal rage?"

I'm suddenly freezing, the outside air biting into my skin. I shake my head, totally lost on what to say. "Teddy, I saw Chris with another girl. I went to see you last Sunday, and they were together in the elevator. She's the same one who's been calling him, and they were together. You were right about him."

"You mean Maria?"

"Do you know her?" I raise my voice, confused. Simone

comes over to see why I'm getting worked up, standing protectively close to me.

"Coco," my brother says. "Chris came to see *me* last Sunday. He wanted to explain himself to me—to clarify his intentions. And he did, and . . ." Teddy looks down, embarrassed. "I feel like an idiot for acting like I did. I mean, it's not like I haven't hooked up a time or—"

"Please don't elaborate," I say, holding up my hand.

"Sorry," my brother says. "Well, anyway, it ended up sort of cool. Chris asked if I had a girlfriend because he thought I should meet someone. He brought me down a few floors to meet this girl Maria. He thought we'd like each other." Teddy grins. "And we do. We've been hanging out. She's the one I'm getting the ticket for, actually."

Stunned, I stand there as Teddy runs his hand through his hair. "I swear," he says. "Chris was like some deranged cupid. You must have dropped off the food when we were down in her room. And then I guess you saw them when she was walking him out. I thought you knew."

"Deranged cupid?" My heart squeezes tight as the realization settles in. "Yeah," I say, running my palm over my face. "That sounds like Chris. And no, he didn't tell me. I sort of— well, I sort of freaked out and told him to never call me again. I thought he was hooking up with her."

Next to me Simone murmurs something close to "Oh,

snap" before stepping to my brother's side like they're about to have an intervention.

My brother's jaw practically hits the ground. "Caroline," he says, taking my shoulders. He sounds exactly like my father. "That guy is nuts for you. And I think I might *actually* mean nuts. He had a whole speech prepared for me—a *speech*, Coco. Who does that? Did you seriously dump him?"

I shrug, feeling heartbroken but maybe a little hopeful. "I thought you hated him," I say in a small voice.

"No." Teddy shakes his head. "Not anymore. And if I knew you were torturing him, I would have told you sooner. Why would you be so stubborn? Why not just ask him what he was doing there?"

"Because . . ." I pause and look up at him. "I ran away instead. Dumb, huh?"

"For the record," Phil says from behind us, "I still hate Chris Drake." When I turn to him, he smiles. "He could do so much better than a nut like you." I reach over to punch his arm. When I flip back around, I find Simone watching me.

"So, Linus," she starts with a smile. "What do you want to do about Joel Ryder?" I only realize then that Joel's already gone inside. Simone adds, "I'm not sure he can compete with Cupid."

"No, I don't think he can. Of course, Chris might hate my guts and never want to speak to me again, but I don't think that's a good enough reason to hang out with Joel."

Simone nods and then reaches to pull me into a hug. "Remember that time I told you to start fighting for yourself?" she says close to my ear. "This is one of those times. There will always be other Freakshows."

I straighten, smiling at my best friend before taking a deep breath, preparing like I'm about to jump off a cliff. "Guess I should make a call," I say, almost hoping she has a better idea.

"I guess you should. I'll take the gang and meet you inside." She smiles. "Or not, depending on your plans."

"Please pray to the gods of broken relationships for this to turn out okay."

She laughs. "I will. And hey"—she points to the moon—"there's a full moon tonight, so weird shit is bound to happen." Simone winks and then turns to grab my sister by the arm to lead her inside, content with Natalie as her replacement wing-woman.

"You're going to call him and apologize?" Teddy asks mockingly. "Wow, Coco—you're so mature."

"Bite me."

Teddy laughs and reaches to tug on the end of my ponytail before he turns to disappear into the crowd to meet the others inside. I'm freezing but too nervous to even feel it at this point.

My heart is pounding in my chest as I consider what the best way to grovel and beg for forgiveness would sound like. I can tell Chris about my sister and Phil—hoping he finds it funny. Or maybe even go the sympathy route and tell him about the fight at school last week. I quickly drop that idea, deciding that funny hurts a lot less to talk about. When I have a solid "Hey there, handsome" opener, I dial Chris's number.

The phone picks up on the first ring, startling me. He doesn't say anything, but I know he's there because I can hear him breathing. His caller ID just totally wrecked my game, and I begin talking before I can even stop myself.

"I'm an idiot and I'm sorry," I say. Wow, not the best start. *Silence.*

"Yes," I say, not sure where to go if he's going to be so unresponsive. "I should have asked what you were doing with Maria instead of running off. I assumed the worst, and for that I'm so sorry. I should have called you sooner—I wanted to—but I was too scared. And I'm scared right now because all I want is for you to say something so I don't ramble on and make this even more awkward." I pause, lowering my voice when a few people walk past me on the sidewalk. "Christopher?"

"Why can't you just trust me?" he asks, low and controlled. "I've never lied to you. Why do you always assume the worst?"

Straight to the point. I forget the cute things I wanted to say, the jokes that would break the tension. Instead I feel the tears sting my eyes, the truth so much harder to say.

"I guess I expect to be disappointed. To *be* disappointing. That's how I felt for a long time, and when my gram died—I thought the best parts of me died with her. You asked what I was crying about that night at the party, and I've never told you. It wasn't just that my gram was gone; it was because I wasn't there for her when she needed me most. And I've spent more than a month hating myself for it. I tried to start over, but I couldn't escape the guilt.

"But then there was you. Your terrible jokes and your quiet singing. Your beautiful eyes and the way you try to fix things. I was wrong—you don't disappoint me. You amaze me." I sniffle, wiping the warm tears that slide down my cheeks. "God, Christopher," I say. "I'm so stupid in love with you that I don't even know what to do about it most of the time. Can't you just—"

"Caroline," he cuts in. I close my eyes, waiting for him to berate me. Tell me that I'm a bad girlfriend and maybe an even worse friend. "I am horribly in love with you, too."

He doesn't go on, and he doesn't have to. Right now, all I want is to see him strumming his guitar, talking carelessly about anything and everything. I just want him.

"You still there?" I ask, wrapping my arms around myself against the cold wind.

"Mm-hmm. But, hey, can you not break up with me again? I ended up reinjuring my leg running after you."

"Bad?" I ask, feeling awful.

"Kind of," he replies. "But I'm sure it's nothing a crime fighter can't fix."

"Oh my God. I am never wearing that again."

"We'll see."

"Can you still drive?" I ask. "I think I'm going to bail on this Electric Freakshow concert, and maybe we can play fight in your room or something. This time I'll have the advantage."

"Electric Freakshow?" He groans. "Caroline, you can do so much better."

I laugh. "All right, Mr. Music Major. Can you come and get me or not?"

"I'm already on my way."

NINETEEN

STAY

"Let's go," Chris says, motioning toward the exit after we retrieve Emma from the bathroom. She's got the bleeding under control, but she's still holding a wad of paper towels under her nose just in case. We follow Chris; he makes a call to whoever else he was with and explains the situation.

Outside, the winter air blasts me in the face, making my cheeks tingle and waking me up inside. I suck in the cold air and it stings my lungs, but I hold it there before I let it out.

"Tell me about yourself," Chris says quietly as we walk. "I mean, other than the stuff that's posted online."

"I hate the song 'Sweet Caroline,' so don't sing it."

He grins. "I can do better." We stop at the car, and I look and notice the moon for the first time tonight—so big and full that it casts everything in a hazy, gray glow. I meet Chris's eyes over the hood of his car, and he winks. Natalie and Emma get into the backseat, Emma saying that she hopes her nose isn't going to be crooked.

But I pause and glance back at the concert arena. I was supposed to be here with Joel; I was supposed to be happy with Joel. Except that I've been miserable with him. Gram told me to be careful who I love—to never give them too much. I see now that maybe she was warning me about the sort of situation that happened with Joel.

And although I've spent the last week sure that Gram would be ashamed of me, I remind myself now that this is *Gram* I'm thinking about. She'd love me no matter what.

I climb in the passenger side and Chris cranks the heat, letting the car warm up. I watch him, studying his expression, his movements. He's so different from Joel, and somehow that's so comforting that when he looks over and smiles warmly, I lean my head back against the seat and just smile back.

Natalie must have noticed my easy rapport with Chris during the ride to the hospital because when we pull up at the ER drop-off, she shocks me by cutting me loose.

"You can go back to the show," she offers.

"I . . . ," I begin, glancing at Chris. He's not even trying to hide his elation. "I'm not interested in going back," I say. Chris's face falls a bit. "But I don't really want to hang out at the hospital either," I quickly add, and turn to Chris. "Can you drive me to Clinton?"

"You're staying at Dad's tonight?" Natalie asks, confused.

"I'll call him and see if I can," I say. "Chris lives in Clinton— he goes to school there."

"Oh, I see," Nat says, nodding. "And that's cool with both of you?"

Chris and I nod like bobble heads, and she leaves to help Emma. I roll down the window and call after her.

"Nat!" She turns and faces me. "I'll tell Dad you're staying tonight too. Just call him when you're done here so he can come get you."

"I will. And thanks," she says, smiling. "Even with all this," she says, waving at the ER behind her, "it was one of my favorites ever."

"Mine too," I say. Then, "I love you, Natalie."

"I love you, too, Caroline," she says easily. "See you soon."

I glance over at Chris; the look on his face is nothing but sweet. Resolved, I wave good-bye to my sister and let him drive us away.

The first snow of the year starts falling just as we pull onto the highway. It's a light dusting: the kind that makes you want to sip cocoa by the fire, not the kind that forces you to stock up on supplies. Chris cranks up the heat another notch and I relax into the headrest. It's strange how you can meet someone and they can make you feel lighter—the stress I've been carrying isn't completely gone, but it's not so heavy right now.

Like someone cut the strap on my backpack of bricks.

I watch the sign that says CLINTON 43 MILES float by in the hazy air. With the full moon so bright, it's hard to see the stars, but I search for them anyway.

"See any constellations?" Chris asks quietly. "I have a telescope in my room if you want to—" He stops and looks over sheepishly. "Not that I'm trying to get you back to my room. I just—"

I laugh. "I think I can see the Big Dipper," I say, touching my finger to the glass, "and Orion. But now that it's snowing, it's all fading into white."

"I love the snow," Chris says, dreamlike.

"Me too," I say, matching his tone. I look from the sky to the road and realize that it's snowing a little harder now as we start to climb the mountain toward Clinton. The headlights spotlight the flakes as they fly in diagonally from left to right. Chris passes a semi with its hazards flashing.

My phone buzzes. I pull it out of my pocket and look to see who it's from. Joel. I delete it without reading the message. Chris goes around another couple of semitrucks, glancing over.

"Your boyfriend?" he asks, nodding to the phone.

"No," I answer automatically. Then, because it's not exactly the truth, I look over at him. "At least not anymore."

Chris grins. "Well, I am incredibly glad to hear that."

"Me too." We settle into a comfortable silence before Chris gets fidgety and begins to tap his thumbs on the steering wheel—to "Sweet Caroline."

"You doing anything exciting for Thanksgiving?" he asks, changing lanes to go around a car with its hazard lights on.

"No," I say. "Not really. I'm supposed to go to my mother's, but I don't know. I might hang at my dad's instead. I haven't spent a holiday with him in like five years." I stop, surprised I'm telling this to a stranger, but Chris just nods along like he doesn't find it even the least bit odd.

"My parents are on a cruise," he says with a laugh. "They invited me, but hanging out on deck chairs while my mother sips gin and tonics just doesn't feel festive to me. A few friends and I are going to hit up Denny's or something." He looks over. "You're welcome to join us."

"Uh, Denny's is gross. Do you want to . . ." I pause, my cheeks reddening. "Do you want to meet my dad?" I ask, laughing to myself as I do. He widens his eyes.

"First I'm trying to get you back to my room, and now you want me to meet your dad? Maybe we should be looking at engagement rings, Caroline."

I melt a little at the way he says my name. "Okay, but make

sure the rock is *huge*," I tell him. "I want everyone to know just how shallow we are."

"Of course." Chris's brow furrows as we get stuck behind yet another eighteen wheeler with its hazards on. "Guess Friday night is hot for hauling," Chris says, nodding to the truck in front of us. "What do you think that tri-axle's got in the wagon, buddy?"

"You speak Trucker?" I ask, laughing.

"I've played trucker video games," he says, "so yes, that makes me fluent." Then, glancing in the rearview mirror, "There's a tanker yanker in our back door coming in hot."

I turn to see what he's talking about. "Tanker yanker. Is that a truck that hauls tanks, by any chance?"

"I have no idea," Chris admits. "I was just trying to impress you with my mad trucking skills."

I cup my hand, pretending it's a CB, and talk into it. "What's your handle, boss man?" I've played the video game in question with Teddy before. I drive a mean triple trailer.

Chris takes a hand off the wheel and cups it over his mouth. He makes a crackling sound into it, then answers me. "Ten four. Handle's Big Daddy; same back atcha. Over."

I roll my eyes at his ridiculous trucker nickname and rack my brain for something cooler. But apparently Chris thinks I'm taking too long because he radios in again. "Don't spend our whole flip-flop trying to one-up me. Over."

I'm about to tell him to get out of the granny lane when I glance up ahead and see, through what's become much heavier snowfall, a long string of brake lights. It strikes me as odd because I know this road and there's no reason to slow down up there: It's where the hill flattens out and runs straight for a few miles before it drops down into the valley where Clinton's nestled. We're coming up on the lights fast, and Chris hits the brakes, but we skid a little on the snow, so he eases off and begins to pump them. Never for one second am I afraid that he'll lose control. I'm calm.

He's calming.

"Wonder what's going on," he mutters as he coaxes the car down to forty instead of sixty. The whole line of lights is in the right lane; he moves into the left so we can go around.

"Mud Flap Madge," I exclaim as we start to pass one of the vehicles stopped on the right, proud of myself.

"Good one," Chris says, squinting a little at the road ahead.

"I totally bested your handle," I say, laughing.

"Roger that," he says with a nod and a quick smile before his eyes are back on the road.

I roll my head to the right, watching the stopped cars and trucks go by, then I reach to turn on the radio. An Electric Freakshow song starts playing, and when I hear the song, sadness wraps around me—reminding me that it was never really gone.

No right answer; perfect marks . . . It's no big deal; it's just your heart . . . Falling stars and lightning sparks . . . This will only sting a bit . . .

"God, I hate this song," Chris says absently, still focused on the road.

"It used to be one of my favorites," I say, thinking that Joel may have ruined EF for me forever. I click off the radio, earning a quick look from Chris. What was fun and carefree is suddenly heavy and suffocating. It's like a shift in not just mood but . . . everything. I glance once more at the moon, feeling unsettled, and then lean forward to watch the road intently.

And then just as we crest the hill and start down into the valley, I suck in all the air in the car—all the air in the world.

Perfectly obscured by Mother Nature and its sideways positioning is a jackknifed tractor trailer blocking the entire two left lanes of the highway. There's no doubt in my mind: We're going to hit the truck.

Instinctively, I know we have to turn.

I reach over to grab the wheel, hoping it'll be enough.

NINETEEN

GO

I climb out of Chris's car in the visitors' parking lot—the student parking was full—and he looks me over with a serious expression as he gets his crutches from the backseat. When I start to apologize again for breaking up with him, he shakes his head.

"Not that," he says, coming to a stop right in front of me. He reaches to zip my Clinton hoodie up to my neck. "I can't believe you own one of their T-shirts."

I laugh, unzipping it a little so that I can breathe. "You're such a hater," I say. "What is your deal with them, anyway?"

"Electric Freakshow is mediocre," he says. "And you are better than mediocre. Even if I'm still a little pissed at you." He doesn't smile because he means it; he doesn't smile, and I miss that part of him so much that I lean forward and put my forehead on his chest, my arms around his waist, and whisper again that I'm sorry.

Chris puts his warm hand on the back of my neck protectively, running his thumb gently over my skin. "I know you are. And I can love you and be pissed at the same time. They're not mutually exclusive."

I straighten and his hand falls away. I think about that statement, that he can love me and be angry, and I realize that I never thought of it that way. All the time I spent feeling like my family hated me, was disappointed in me—they still loved me. I was too stubborn—scared—to see it. I've wasted so much time.

"I'm going to stay at my dad's," I tell Chris. "At least until I go to college. I like it there."

"I'm glad you'll be close. Easier for me to stalk you that way." He leans down on his crutch to give me a soft peck, reminding me of the first time he kissed me over orange chicken. We start walking, commenting on the bright white snow that's started to fall. I nearly slip once on a patch of ice.

"Be careful," he says, reaching out to steady me. "Both of us on crutches would just be too pathetic." We stop at the crosswalk, and I push the button for the walking man to tell us when to go.

"By the way." I turn to him. "I can't believe you set my brother up with Maria." I feel a small pinch of jealousy, but I decide this time to trust him—to let myself be vulnerable so that I don't lose him.

"They're good for each other," Chris says, rubbing his hands over my arms to warm me up. "I'll set up your sister too, if you want. Ed needs a new—"

"Gross," I say with a laugh. "Ed is done licking my friends." Apparently Simone and Ed met up after dealing with Teddy that day. Her retelling—charades style—was cringe inducing. Just then the light changes, and Chris and I start to cross the street.

"Are we still on for Thanksgiving at my mom's?" I ask. "I neglected to tell her about our breakup."

He glances over. "Is it because you were secretly hoping we'd get back together?"

I shake my head but then smile. "Actually, yeah. I probably was. Either way, I'm sure she'll find you adorably obnoxious."

"Tell me again how crazy you are about me," Chris says, his eyes narrowed in a way that makes me think our fighting has come to an end.

My stomach flutters, and I stop to turn to him. "Christopher Drake," I call out dramatically, loudly so that other people can hear me. Embarrassment will make it count more. "I'm totally crazy in love with you—"

I notice the light slide across his face, setting off the bright blue of his eyes. I furrow my brow, not sure where it's coming from, when Chris's expression falls. He's about to shout as he reaches for my arm, and I turn to look over my shoulder. A car is gliding in our direction—fishtailing on a patch of ice as it tries to brake for the light.

Chris pulls me to the side, but it's not soon enough. He's standing still, but I'm flying: first onto the metal of the hood and then, when the brakes finally work, into the air. My limbs fling out in zero gravity; my arm connects with concrete, the pain sharp and blinding. Then my head hits, sending me into darkness.

TWENTY

STAY

"What are you, pain intolerant?" Chris jokes as the nurse sews another stitch into my forehead. The spot is numbed from painkillers, but still, I'm sure it looks nasty. I don't move my head, but I let my gaze fall on Chris's face, and when I do, I see in his blue eyes concern so true it's painful.

"It could've been so much worse," I say. He's on crutches—he dislocated his knee when the car impacted with the mile marker right outside his door—and he shifts to lean on the left. Finally his eyes find mine again.

"I'm sorry for trying to kill you," he says, looking sheepish.

"Was it because I like Electric Freakshow?"

"Yes, you got me," he says, laughing a little. "I am trying to off their fans, one member at a time, until the band is forced to stop touring. It's my evil plan, but I've been thwarted."

"I'm an excellent thwarter." The nurse laughs quietly at us. We stop talking for a moment.

"If I promise not to try to kill you again, will you go out on a real date with me?" Chris asks. He looks adorably pathetic.

I open my mouth to respond when my parents—both of them, together—rush in.

"Oh my God, Caroline," my mom says, seeing the blood on my shirt. Chris crutches away a few steps so they can get close to me—they're too focused on me to notice him at all.

"It's just a scratch," I say. "Head wounds bleed a lot, even if they're nothing, right?" I look at the nurse expectantly.

"That's right," she says, smiling. "She only needed ten stitches." Then, repeating what I said to Chris, she adds, "It could've been much worse."

"I should have checked the weather," my dad says. "I should have gotten a hotel room for you and your sister in the city so you wouldn't have been out on the roads."

"Dad, come on," I say. "It's just a scratch."

"But what if . . ." His voice cracks and his words trail off. I watch as my parents look at each other—really look at each other—both of them probably envisioning losing a child.

I glance over at Chris as he hobbles to the window. "Oh!" my mom says, seeing him for the first time. "Who's this?"

In the moment I realize that I don't know his last name,

Chris steps in. He makes his way over and, when he seems stable, offers my parents a hand in turn. "Chris Drake," he says. "It's very nice to meet you."

"You look familiar," my mom says, smiling. "Have we met before?"

"It's possible," Chris says, darting a playful look at me. "Caroline and I go way back."

Maybe way back to another life—maybe that's why I'm so comfortable with you, I think.

My parents pump Chris for information about his life—his major, where he grew up, his hobbies—and I listen, taking mental notes for later. After a while, a friend comes to get him and we're forced to say good-bye—in front of his friend and my parents.

He comes over for a hug.

"Our meeting tonight, it feels a little like fate, doesn't it?" he whispers into my ear.

"Well, you did say you stalked me," I say. "So maybe it feels more like . . . perseverance? And of course, there was the attempted murder."

He chuckles, pulling back so the hug doesn't linger into the inappropriate-in-front-of-parents zone. "Well, whatever the reason, I'm glad we met."

"Me too," I say, meaning it. And when Chris crutches away, I realize that I wish he didn't have to. I wish he'd stay.

• • •

Late at night, I'm in bed at Mom's when my cell buzzes. I wasn't asleep—the painkillers have worn off and my head is throbbing. I reach over and read Joel's text in the dark.

WHAT HAPPENED TO YOU?

For some reason, the question makes me laugh. I think back on the last six weeks of my life and really, what *didn't* happen to me? I stare at the screen, thumbs ready to type, feeling like I'm experiencing a moment—one of those moments when the decision you make really matters. I type: CAN YOU TALK?

Joel doesn't reply, but my phone rings a few minutes later. It's middle-of-the-night hushed on his end except for the whispered lyrics to "Flannel" playing in the background. Like I've been through war and somehow come out unscathed, I'm numb to its power. All it is right now is the absence of silence.

"Hi," I say quietly. "Thanks for calling."

"No problem," he says, matching my low tone. He waits, and then, "This is it, right, Caroline?"

"Yes." We listen to the part in the song about forever love.

"I'm sorry," he says, and I wonder for which part. Then I realize that none of this was his fault. At no point in our relationship was Joel anything other than himself.

At lots of points, though, I was.

"I'm sorry too."

"This didn't turn out how I thought it would," he admits.

"Me either," I say, but I'm not sure if it's the truth or just a statement meant to make him feel better. "Well . . ."

"Yeah."

"Hey, Joel?"

"Yeah?"

"Thanks."

"For what?" he asks. I hear him shift in his bed. In the bed that changed me.

"Thank you for sharing a little bit of your life with me."

He laughs once, quietly, then, "That's a cool thing to say, Caroline. You're a cool girl. And . . . you're welcome. Thank you for doing the same."

We say good-bye and when I hang up, I feel lifted for having had the conversation. It would've been easy to float on as Joel's girlfriend for a while longer—to enjoy the win—and just as easy to end it with a text. But he let me in. He showed me his insides. He shared things that were difficult for him to share—he opened up. And for that, I owed him the courtesy of my voice. I owed him a proper ending.

Afterward, my head doesn't hurt as much.

My heart doesn't hurt as much.

I inch down deep under the comforter and exhale, watching through the break in the curtains as huge flakes fall outside. For the first time in a long time, I don't think of what's happened—only what's to come. And with hope and possibility whispering me a lullaby, I sleep.

TWENTY

GO

The sound of a guitar filters into my ears, tender and slow and all for me. "Sweet Caroline," he sings softly, only it's not the Neil Diamond version. It's mine. "Blindsided by you . . . I never really knew how good it could be . . . my sweet, sweet Caroline. . . ."

"Stop being cute," I murmur as I wake up. I turn to see Chris next to me in the hospital chair, the same place he's sat for close to a week. "It's Thanksgiving," I tell him. "You should be with your family." I try to sit up, tangling myself in the tubes attached to my hand.

"First of all," he says, setting his guitar aside, "I wasn't going to leave you after surgery. Secondly, I have no interest in going to the Bahamas with my parents right now. My mom said she hopes you're feeling better, by the way."

Chris's eyes meet mine, still guilt-ridden as if it's his fault

I got hit by a car on an icy road. As I hold his gaze, he reaches to run his fingers down my arm until they touch the cast just below my elbow, then back up again. The bones in my left arm were shattered, and so once my vitals stabilized, they operated—putting my arm back together with pins and metal rods. Teddy's been calling me RoboCop.

"Those goddamn crutches," Chris mutters. "I couldn't get traction when I tried to grab you. I—" His face breaks like he might cry, and I take him by the collar of his T-shirt and pull him to me.

"It's not your fault," I whisper near his ear. "So stop blaming yourself." I think about how I felt after Gram died, how I wished I could have done it differently. But you can't live with guilt. You can't let it take everything that's you.

My mother walks in, and Chris straightens out of my arms, sniffling hard. Mom is holding a stack of Tupperware, a bag dangling from her wrist as Juju totters in behind her. My father and brother have already left, promising to come back later, so this is my official Thanksgiving dinner with my mom. In a hospital room.

"I hope you like yams, Christopher," she says. "They're very good for you." He shoots me a look and crinkles his nose but then stands to help my mother.

"If you made them, I'm sure they're delicious," he says. He takes the food from her hands and hops over to set it on the side table. It wasn't the best of circumstances for them to meet, him frantically calling her from the hospital, but after the first day I kind of like the way she is around him. She's very . . . motherly.

Juju sets her sippy cup on my white blanket before trying to yank the IV tube from my hand. "No, no," my mother says sweetly to her. "That'll hurt Coco." She busies my little sister with her cell phone, and Juju makes her way to the hospital chair on the other side of the bed.

"Albert is entertaining your aunt Claudia at the moment," Mom says, pulling some paper plates out of the bag. "We should probably include him in our prayers." When she smirks, I choke out a laugh, surprised that my mother can be sarcastically funny when I'm laid up in a hospital bed. I think we're more alike than I realized.

"There's no silverware," Chris says after everything is unpacked. "I'll grab some from the cafeteria." He grabs his crutches and leaves. When he's gone, my mom turns to me. "I really like that kid," she says. "He reminds me a lot of your grandfather—sort of goofy, but in that really endearing way."

I smile, her approval of Chris making it feel more real somehow. Maybe it's the holiday spirit or maybe it's the drugs still coursing through me, but as she comes to lay a napkin over my lap, my eyes tear up. "I miss you, Mom," I whisper.

"I miss you, too," she says, reaching to brush my hair away from my face.

"Living with Dad and Debbie," I start, "you know it's not because of you, right?" There's a flash of hurt across her face, but she nods.

"I know you like it there. So long as you come and stay with me sometimes, I'll get over it." The last weight, the last bit of guilt, leaves then. I lay my head back, watching the scene contently. The door opens and Chris reappears with a handful of plastic bags filled with clear silverware.

While Juju is distracted, my mother and Chris pull up chairs as we share a meal. Mom can't stay long, so Chris and I indulge in pumpkin cheesecake alone as she gathers up her things. Despite the fact that I'm in the hospital, she still has her own Thanksgiving to lead at her house.

"Thanks for the food, Mom," I say as she comes over to give me a kiss good-bye. "And the company."

She smiles, looking as thrilled as I've ever seen her. "Anytime, Coco," she says. "I'll be back in the morning." She says good-bye to Chris and then takes Judith's outstretched hand and leads her out of the room, closing the door behind them.

Once they're gone, Chris sets his drink aside and then comes over to ease onto the bed next to me. He lifts my unbroken arm to take my hand and kiss my fingers.

"Those yams were disgusting," he murmurs. "I'm just lucky she didn't make me try that green bean casserole."

"Maybe at Christmas," I say, closing my eyes as Chris

kisses my shoulder through the hospital gown. "Or New Year's." I'm a little breathless as his lips touch my neck, his kisses sweet and mostly innocent—unlike my thoughts. "Easy now, we're in a hospital," I joke.

"I'm going to get under the covers with you, okay?" His voice is serious.

"Okay."

Chris climbs in, curling around me as I snuggle close. It's only a minute before I feel the first shudder, hear his sniffle as his tears fall on my skin. I thread my fingers through his blond hair and say nothing. He doesn't talk—maybe can't talk—for a long time. His arms are locked around me like a vise, his breath warm as he buries his face in my hair.

"I was so scared," he whispers eventually. "First at the accident—you were so still, it was like you were gone." He chokes up. "Then waiting for you to wake up, your surgery. Caroline, I can't handle the idea of losing you. I can't—"

"Stop," I say, pulling back so I can look at him. "I'm here. Just like fate, remember? You couldn't lose me if you tried."

Chris rests on his elbow, gazing down at me. His eyes are bloodshot but still so blue. He puts his palm on my cheek, checking me over one last time before he leans down to kiss me—telling me to stay, stay with him—and to never run away again.

EPILOGUE

Simone, Natalie, and I are splayed out on the couch on a summer Sunday, watching an interview on E! with River Devlin about his stint in rehab and the collapse of Electric Freakshow.

"I can't believe this is happening," Natalie says through fingertips, as if the breakup of our favorite band is on par with a national disaster. "They were so good together."

"All good things must come to an end," Simone says ominously.

"Not *all* good things," I say, smiling as I think of Chris.

"Vomit," Simone says good-naturedly. I throw a piece of popcorn at her—which she dodges, then eats—and refocus on the TV. The interviewer is asking about examples of times when there were differences of opinion among band members.

"There were too many to count," River says, shifting in his chair and tossing back his hair like it's a tic more than a necessity. "But I mean, like, take 'Magnets for Fate.' Huge hit, right?"

The interviewer nods. "I should say so—it spent a year in the top five."

"Right," River says, his voice gravelly. "That was one that I wrote, and I still to this day don't think Nicky and Argent even got it. I've seen them out there, talking about what it meant to them, and they totally missed the fu—"

Beep.

"—point, man."

It makes me like him more for calling the gorgeous host "man."

"Yes, I've seen the interviews in question," she says, and it comes off like she's trying to prove that she did her home-work. "It seems like the song's message is that all of us are living a life set out for us by destiny. By fate."

River slams his hand to his knee. "No, man!" he says, running his hands through his too-long hair. "That's what I mean! No one gets it. But they buy it. They spend their allow-ance to download it. And yet they have no idea what they're singing along to."

"Why don't you explain it to us, then?" the interviewer says, clearly annoyed.

"I don't think I should have to," River says, shifting again. The interviewer looks at him expectantly. "Fine," he says. "It's just . . . the point is that yeah, we're fated to live a certain life. But it's not like we're being mind controlled or something. There's a little thing called free will."

"So you're saying we have control over our lives?" the interviewer asks. "That we can change our fate?"

"I'm saying we have freedom to make mistakes," River says, shaking his head. "I'm saying that our mistakes—one mistake or many of them—don't define us. They don't derail us. We end up where we need to be in the end." He pauses. "But hopefully having learned something from our stumbles . . . having grown into better people because of them."

"It seems like we're saying the same thing here." The interviewer reaches over and takes a sip from an Electric Freakshow mug.

River gets a funny look on his face. "Is that coffee?" he asks. She nods. He laughs to himself, and I imagine that I know what he's thinking . . . about the lyrics at the end of "Magnets for Fate."

And no matter where you sit, how fast you sip . . . The coffee tastes the same on magnet lips.

River stands and pulls out his microphone; with a stunned interviewer gawking after him, he walks off the stage.

"Well, that'll earn him some headlines tomorrow," Simone says. "Pure publicity stunt."

"I can't believe he just did that," Natalie says, like she's his mother and she's disappointed in him. She and Simone start chatting about how River used to be so much nicer in interviews and I zone out, getting it. Getting him.

For some reason, in that moment, I think of the night Gram died. I think of how Simone offered me the choice to stay or go—and how it so easily could have gone the other way. For a moment, I wonder what life would look like had I gone down the other path. But then I think of River Devlin and what he was trying to say. He wasn't saying that I'd end up in the same place either way so it didn't matter. He was trying to say that whatever life I lived because of the choice I made is important. And maybe I found my way back to basically the same place—who really knows—but the mistakes I made make me who I am.

We may be drawn to our fates like magnets, but whatever we pick up along the way means something. Mistakes mean something.

"I have to go call Chris," I say, standing from the couch. "I'll be right back."

I run upstairs to my room and shut the door, then instead of calling Chris, I write the first piece of fan mail ever in my life. I write about the night Gram died. I write about my life ever since. And who knows if River Devlin will see it. Who knows if he'll even care. But in that moment, I need to tell him that I spent my allowance downloading a song that I love—but also one that I understand.

. . .

Four weeks later, I open my e-mail and nearly have a heart attack.

Waiting there above a forwarded viral video from Simone and a love note from Chris is a message from The. River. Devlin. Or, I think cynically, *whoever writes e-mails for him.* But when I open the message—when I see the content—I know it's authentic. I know he wrote it. It's five words, written like they're a continuation of a conversation. No hello. No good-bye. Just a glimpse into his mind. Just enough to hear "thank you" even when he didn't say it.

I sit there awhile, smiling, reading the words over and over again:

You made the right choice.

ACKNOWLEDGMENTS

The authors would like to thank the following people:
Their agents, Dan Lazar and Jim McCarthy.
Fabulous editor Jennifer Klonsky.
Much-loved Liesa Abrams,
and the entire team at Simon Pulse.
Their author networks, dear friends, and families
near and far . . . especially, as always, their grandmothers.